Geordie Boy
by
Tony Hunt

Stories about small events in a child's life

'I cannot think of any need in childhood as strong as the need for a father's protection.'

Sigmund Freud

These short stories concern the growing up of a small boy on a council estate in the North East of England just after the end of the second world war.

That small boy is probably me. Many of the incidents did happen: some have been modified, some airbrushed; some have simply been invented – and it is for those of you who know me to work out which is which. Others who come across this snapshot might look at the incidents I recount and ask what might have been.

As you read the stories, I hope that you will notice the boy's constant search for role models – good or bad. You will be able to notice how he, in the absence of immediate familial support, seems to seek validation in various ways by being involved in different activities and by encountering various people, some good, some very dubious. Nothing strange or unusual there at all.

Yet, I hope that you will also see that the pressures and events that led to the disintegration of the boy's family, although tiny and in many ways, insignificant, had a huge cumulative effect. These small tragedies made everything so much more difficult for everyone – and sapped any humour and joy from the lives of many people for a very long time.

And this, if there is one, is the main point of the book – what might have been. Part of me is that small boy, and I have enjoyed my life tremendously – so far. I did eventually get a good education and have made a reasonable living. I have five wonderful children who have all become successful in their chosen careers. But it all could have been so much easier. And being easier it might have led to far better outcomes.

A word about the final story in this collection: it is, appropriately I think, the 'back story'. It is the context in which the events themselves happened. The coincidences, the demographic shift caused by two world wars – the sheer chance that brought certain players together – this cocktail of circumstances is what caused me to want to write this collection.

Nevertheless, I must never forget that this is a 'small' story, and the effect of any of the events that I recount has not altered the way that the planets move. Many of the people who know me will not have known anything of what I write, and indeed, some may well be surprised that I am even mentioning such small issues.

One
Moving to the Marden

I am three years old. I'm standing by the fireplace watching my grandma as she cleans the grate. She's on her knees, so her head is at the same level as mine, and she's putting the ashes on to a sheet of newspaper which she has just rolled up into a little packet. Then she takes some more newspaper and rolls each sheet of newspaper into a sort of long tube and ties it into a knot. These little knots she puts into the hearth and on top of them, she puts some thin sticks of wood which she takes from a small box next to the fireplace.

I know what happens next. When the wood sticks are on top of the knots of newspaper, Grandma takes her little shovel, puts it into the coal scuttle, and adds some small pieces of coal to the newspaper and the sticks. Later in the day, she will take a match out from her matchbox and light the newspaper knots. The newspaper will light the sticks, the sticks will light the coal, and the fire will make us all warm. I know this is true, because she does the same thing every day.

She keeps looking at me as she finishes setting the fire, then, as she gets up, she makes one of those 'Oooohhh' sounds that all grandmas make when they stand up or sit down, and she touches me on the nose with her finger.

'Today is a very special day for you, little man.'

'What Grandma?' I don't know what she means. 'What's my special day?'

'You're going in a car and you will be going to your new house today. As soon as Daddy gets here, he'll be taking you. Your mam's already there, waiting for you. And in your new house you will have your very own room - with a lovely little bed.'

'I like it here, Grandma. I like watching you make the fire.'

'I know you do my pet, but you will be much happier in your new home – and Grandad and me – we'll come and visit you as soon as you have settled in. Daddy's borrowed a car as well, so it's going to be a real adventure for you. You in a car with your daddy – and going to a new house.'

I am puzzled. Me in a car with my daddy? I can't remember if I've ever been in a car before. I've seen cars passing outside the house, and I have two Dinky toy cars of my own – and I can make the engine noises. I don't know what Grandma means by a 'new house' either. I watch her walk through the kitchen and I follow her out to the back door where she lifts the lid off the dustbin and pops the little parcel of ashes into it.

She rinses her hands under the tap in the kitchen, dries them on the tea towel and turns to me. She smiles again, 'Now then pet lamb, what would you like for your dinner? What about a nice little egg and some soldiers?' And she gives me another cuddle, taking my head in both of her hands and ruffling my hair. I like it when she makes me a boiled egg and she knows that, so I don't have to answer. But I'm not really thinking about my dinner, I'm thinking about what my Grandma has been saying about my new house – and about me riding in a car.

I can't remember being in a car of any kind before that day. This was to be my first ever trip in a car, and on the day when we moved to our own house on the brand-new Marden Estate. I couldn't handle the excitement properly; there was too much to take in.

My Daddy's just arrived outside Grandma's house. And there's a car by the gate; he's borrowed it. He told my grandma he was going to borrow one, and we'll be using it to take all our things over to the new house. And I'm going to be sitting in the front seat.

The car is not very big – not like a van or a lorry – so Dad has had to pack everything in very carefully. It's made him quite annoyed, and I've just got a clip around the ear for getting in the way, and my grandma is now cuddling me – she seems to like doing that - and tut-tutting about something.

I think there's more stuff to take than he thought. My dad's just driven off without me, saying there's no room, and he'll be back as quickly as he can. My mam is there already, waiting for me, Grandma tells me once more, but I still don't know where 'there' is.

Because my daddy has driven off, I get my boiled egg after all. I sit at the big table on a cushion, and I make a bit of a mess, but my grandma clears it up quickly with her cloth while she puts the tea on. I get down from the table and move to the kitchen door. Because today is Wednesday, Grandma has put the white tripe into a white dish. She peels and chops an onion – and that makes her cry a little – adds it to the dish, then she pours some milk on the tripe, and sprinkles salt and pepper on it. She puts the white dish into the oven and lights the gas. Then, as she closes the oven door, she turns to me, smiles and says, 'What about a story?'

Too late for the story: my grandad has just got home from work and he seems surprised to see me. Grandad doesn't give me cuddles. He never seems to smile, either. The only things that make him happy are his cigarettes, and as soon as he sits down, he takes out some tobacco and puts it into a little silver thing that he presses, and out comes a cigarette. Mam and Dad don't have machines to make their cigarettes. Their cigarettes come in little packets. My mam smokes 'Player's Navy Cut' and my dad smokes 'Woodbines'. I know that because they want me to be able to read and they have shown me the letters on these packets. I can't read the words, but the pictures are enough for me to know what to say.

'He's still here!' my grandad says to Grandma, looking at me. 'The lad's still here. You promised me they were going today – gone by the time I got home, you said.'

'I know, Frank, I'm sorry.' My grandma seems nervous. She's got a hankie in her hands and she's fiddling with it and tying it into knots.

'Stan couldn't get everything into the car ...'

Stan is my dad. They are talking about him. My Grandad takes his cigarette out of his mouth. He looks angry. He's just about to say something, but Grandma hasn't finished.

'He's taken a full load now, almost everything, and he's coming straight back,' says my grandma. 'There wasn't room for Anthony and all their stuff. He won't be long, Frank. Just a few minutes. He'll be back as soon as he's dropped off everything – he'll be on his way back soon. It won't be long.'

Do they not like me here? My grandma is always cuddling me, she likes me to be here, I know. But Grandad? He's always very quiet; he hardly ever speaks to me, except to tell me off.

***

Of course, there was a reason, probably several reasons why my Grandad was angry. I get it now, but then, I couldn't understand why he was so angry all the time. The main reason was that Wallsend Road was already overcrowded before we moved in, and our arrival – and our subsequent long stay with them had been very difficult for everyone.

The house itself, number four Wallsend Road, didn't belong to Grandma and Grandad. It belonged to a Dr Martin, our family doctor, and as I later found out, they had all ended up living there because of one of the bombing raids on the Tyne shipyards in 1941. North Shields and Tynemouth had been close to the targets of air raids aimed at destroying the shipyards, and my family, as had many others, had been the unintended victims of those raids.

A direct hit on a local church on the corner of Coach Lane had seen her, and everyone else in the immediate vicinity, suddenly made homeless. The local doctor had stepped in, offered the use of a house that he owned, and which was vacant at the time, and my family was given the chance to move from their shop in Stormont Street to Wallsend Road.

Grandma had taken over looking after the shop when Granny became too old to do the work, and my grandad had a full-time job working for the council as a rent collector.

The bombing of the shop traumatised everyone and, of course, any income from it was immediately lost. Not only that, they were now having to pay rent on their new accommodation.

To compound their difficulty, there was yet another family member who was forced into moving to a new house with them after Stormont Street was bombed. This was my Uncle John – great uncle, really – a single man, the youngest son of the family, but a man so tightly tied to his mother's apron strings – even though she was eighty years old – that he had to move with them as well.

Four adults had moved into the house at Wallsend Road, a house with two small double bedrooms and a tiny single upstairs; a sitting room and dining room downstairs. The sitting room was never to be used – only for Christmas Day – and for one other, slightly creepy purpose (can you guess?). Nobody went into it: that was the rule.

And this arrangement had worked well for them. My great granny arrived at her new home, took over the upstairs front bedroom and never came out of it again. My Uncle John had the single room and locked it with a padlock every time he went to work, and my grandma and grandad had the back bedroom to themselves. The downstairs kitchen and dining room were where they sat, ate and welcomed any guests.

And then we arrived – Mam, Dad and me - almost doubling the number of people at the house and throwing the cosy pattern of life that they developed into chaos.

My mam and dad had begun their life together in a small bedsit on Front Street, Tynemouth. When I was born, the landlord evicted them, so with nowhere to go, the three of us ended up having to live at Wallsend Road.

I have lived in many houses with my own growing family. From time to time there have been people who, for whatever reason, needed to live with us for a short time, and I know that even with the best of intentions on both sides, an atmosphere can soon build up.

How and where did my mam, my dad and I fit in? These were old people we had imposed our lives upon, people who were set in their ways. Having a toddler in the house must have been a nightmare for them. Young children cry, nappies must be washed - and dried; those of you who are parents know how much 'stuff' you accumulate. We had to invade the sacrosanct front room, living and sleeping there, but we also had to share the one small upstairs bathroom.

We lived at Wallsend Road for well over two years, and I think that I can understand why my grandad was ready to see the back of us. You will have had people outstay their welcome in your home, and you know how the tension builds up. Here the tension had evidently built up. My grandad was being tipped over the edge.

'He told me they would be away by today, by the time I got back from ma work - ye know I'm right!' I hear my grandad mutter and his strong Glaswegian accent adds an extra threatening tone. 'Today, Stan said – and it was a promise. Bloody man, ye canna trust a word he says!'

I hear the naughty word, I know people shouldn't say these words. My grandma knows I've heard it too.

'Not in front of the boy, Frank. Please. It will only be a few minutes.' My grandad looks at me, turns without saying anything, and starts to make another cigarette.

I've just heard the car pull up outside and a door slam. That's my daddy – he's come for me.

I'm watching my daddy now. He's come into the house and he has a scowl on his face. He didn't say hello to Grandad. He's picked up a big pile of clothes and stuff and he's gone out to the car.

Grandma says to me, 'There, I told you he would come back.' And she smiles.   She's not angry like Grandad – or like my daddy.

She's holding my coat and my hat. My gloves are on a long piece of string in the sleeves of my coat, but I don't put them on. She helps me to button the coat up, and she pulls an itchy woollen hat down over my ears, and gives me a big hug, squashing the breath from me.

'There you are, pet – now you are ready for your adventure.' She smiles, 'Give me a big kiss.' Then she spoils it all by taking her hankie – the one she's been fiddling with all this time, spitting on it, and using her forefinger, she gives my face a rub, as if she was rubbing out something, erasing the dirt. I hate it when she does that and squirm a bit to try to get away.

At that moment, my daddy comes back into the house, picks up another pile of stuff with both hands, turns to me and says, 'Right Son, in the car' We then both walk together, out of the house and towards the car. Daddy doesn't say anything either to Grandad or Grandma, but she calls from the doorstep to me.

'I love you, little man.'

I'm now sitting in the front seat of the car, trying to keep my balance on a big pile of books which has been covered by some clothes. There is also something that is quite hard and sharp that is sticking into me, but I don't know what it is. I don't want to tell my dad about this because he's still looking angry. He's got a cigarette in his mouth and he's not said a word to me since we left my grandma's house.

This means that I am not enjoying my first ever ride in the front seat of a car as much as I thought I would.

Still, I am very excited. They've all been talking about this 'new home' that I am going to live in. I'm going to find out what it is – and I know that my mam is already there waiting for me. I already miss my grandma a bit, though.

Two

Our Brand-New House

'Home sweet home. This is the place to find happiness. If one doesn't find it here, one doesn't find it anywhere.' M K Soni

And there's my mam waiting at the front door. She sees the car, waves to me, and comes out to meet us at the gate. Now she's there – and she's smiling. She's really happy to see me and she picks me up as she pulls open the gate and says, 'Hello Chicken. Welcome to your new home.'

Over the next ten years or so, as things happened one after the other, it soon became apparent that my mother wasn't going to have too much to smile about during her short life (she was dead at forty-seven), and my recollections of times when she was genuinely happy are truly precious – and very few. This was one of those times.   She was in her first family home, and it was brand new. It was a new start, and she was going to make a success of it.

I'm in my mam's arms now, looking around, trying to understand where I am and what is going on around me. Everything is so different from Wallsend Road – and different from any road or street that I have ever seen before. I notice that although our new house looks like a proper house and has a roof on it and windows, and the one next door has people looking out of their front window at us, all the other houses seem to be empty. Some don't have a roof on, some don't even have windows.

'Mam, why are those houses broken?'

'They're not broken, pet, they have not been finished yet. The builders are still building them. But they've done a really special job just for you.'

'Why?'

'I had a quiet word with the builder - the man who's in charge, and I said that my Anthony was coming to live here very soon, and that he would like his bedroom finished very quickly, please.'

'What did the builder man say, Mam?'

'He said he'd put his best workman on the job, and he told him to hurry up about it. So, that's why our house is finished, and your very own bedroom is waiting for you. Do you want to come up and see it, pet?'

'Mac, put the boy down and take these, will you?' Dad was in a hurry. 'I said I'd have this car back by five and it's almost six now.'

He gives my mam the things from the front seat of the car, the books, clothes and stuff that I had been sitting on all the way from Wallsend Road. The pointy thing that made my journey so uncomfortable was a kettle, and that is the last thing Dad hands to my mam.

'I got this too – we don't have one.'

'Stan. that's me mam's kettle! Does she know you've taken it?'

'It's her spare, she doesn't use it – and we don't have one. We need it more than they do. They won't even notice. They can have it back when we're settled. Now I've got to go. Don't wait up.'

'Where are you going?'

'Crescent Club – Cullercoats. I'm playing tonight, and I'll go straight on there when I drop the car off.'

And my dad gets into the car and drives away. He doesn't wave – doesn't look back. Mam looks at the pile of our belongings dumped there on the ground outside the gate. She's not happy now. She was smiling before, but she's not smiling now. She's frowning. She's sad now. But she looks at me again, sees my confusion – where's my dad going - and her face lights up, 'I've got my little soldier with me, haven't I?'

'Yes Mam – that's me. I'm your little soldier.' It's my turn to smile; I like this game.

'You'll look after your mam now, won't you?'

'Yes Mam.' And I will.

Between us, although it is not exactly between 'us' at all - my mam carries most of it, but between us we carry the rest of the stuff that has been emptied from the car on to the pavement outside of the gate, and we take it in through the front door.

One thing I notice, one thing I notice at the age of three, on that day, and it still fascinates me now, is the surface of the pavement on which our things had been dumped. It was a rich red colour. A bright, red kind of tarmacadam had been used for all the pavements on our brand-new Marden Estate. It made the place special for me. I don't recall seeing such pavements anywhere else either.

Once all our stuff is inside the house, my mam closes the front door and then she says, 'Now Anthony, this is your new house. You, Daddy and me, we are the only people who are going to live here – and you, my beautiful little man, you are going to have your very own bedroom. What do you think of that?'

I'm not sure what to think. I don't really know what she means, but she is smiling, so I think it must be something good.

'Can I see - my own bedroom, Mam?'

'See it? Of course, you can, my pet. We will take a tour - a royal tour - so you can see everything you want to see. Come on, little soldier – Attention! Quick – march! Left right, left right. First stop – your bedroom!' And off we march.

The front door of our house opens directly into the combined sitting and dining room. Inside the front door, there is a sort of glass cubicle arrangement to keep the weather out when the door is opened. Through it we march, me following my mam as she leads the troops – me. The staircase is just ahead of us and we don't even break step as we mount the staircase and march up the stairs into my bedroom – into my very own bedroom.

Our house, one of the first to be let for occupancy on the Marden Estate, was a two-bedroomed semi-detached property, with a small garden to the front and another small garden at the rear.

My room was the house's second bedroom; Mam and Dad had the one overlooking the front. Right next to my bedroom door was the door to our little bathroom and for just over one year, that bedroom of our first house was my own. It became my den, my castle, my play pen – my prison when the hairbrush came out and I was spanked and sent to it, and the place where me and Louis Sparks would, on one occasion, take all our clothes off and dance around.

When my sister Glenda arrived a year after we had moved in, my very own bedroom soon had to be shared, and it was not until we moved to our next council house further up towards the top of the Marden, on Stanton Road, that I managed to get my own room back once again.

The back windows of our little kitchen, the dining room and my bedroom looked out on to open fields behind, and for a couple of years or so, we could play out in these fields, exploring as far as the disused quarry on some occasions. We didn't go there too often, as bigger boys played there, and there was also a sense of dread about the place. Its deep waters were scary to little boys, so we generally stayed away.

But we had the choice: we could play outside on the street, or we could play in the fields. Nobody seemed to worry about us, and (this is not just nostalgia talking) nobody got hurt, abducted or assaulted either. Kids played out - that's what kids did. And they came in when it got dark.

The fields that we enjoyed playing in so much were soon to be filled by row upon row of semi-detached private houses. And, as I spent a lot of time in my bedroom, looking out of my window, I became something of an expert on the building trade as, over the next few months, I watched all that construction going on behind our house.

I used to sit at my window when I got home from school and watch the builders at work, and in the evenings, after I had been sent to bed, I would watch the older boys climbing on the scaffolding and larking about. Soon I would be able to do that, and I couldn't wait.

The people who were building the properties immediately behind my house were not commercial builders. These houses were the 'self-builds', and a group of enthusiastic amateur builders, carpenters, plumbers and electricians began to create their own houses, moving from one to another as each development was completed.

The kids from these houses were soon to join us at our school, and the circle of boys and girls from which we could draw our friends – and of course, our enemies, began to take shape. Territory, turf wars, gangs – all this began in earnest. The saving grace is that we were all no more than about five years old, so the level of threat that we posed to society was probably not too significant.

All the new houses in our street came with their own separate wash house too. Down the path at the side of our house and across from the back-kitchen door was a small brick shed, purpose built and set up to be used as a laundry.

Combined with the unique red pavement outside, this wash house convinced me that my new home was very special indeed. I haven't seen many council houses with this kind of facility; I am sure that our estate was not unique, but a purpose-built laundry, complete with all the equipment provided by the council, was a truly special feature.

It had running water and a deep Belfast sink, a brand-new Sheila's maid hung from the ceiling and there was a huge iron mangle next to the gas-heated boiler – and even the boiler had its own 'posser' – that thing that allowed you to agitate the washing while it was in the boiler. Remember, this was long before washing machines came along.

The council even provided a proper washing line in the back garden, strung between two poles, along with a long wooden prop to hold the washing line up. That prop often found itself being used for a variety of different purposes – mostly the product of the imaginations of small and mischievous minds.

Nowadays an enterprising person could probably have started a successful laundry business from that wash house, but I don't think that my mam ever thought along those lines. Very soon, the room was too full of rubbish to be used for anything like its intended purpose.

Anything that we weren't using in the house, or that had been broken and needed fixing, anything 'spare' or that would 'come in handy' would find itself joining the ever-increasing pile of miscellaneous rubbish that rendered the wash house unusable for anything except those children's games which involved hiding and dressing up.

In subsequent domestic patterns that my mam developed in her other houses, the absence of a wash house required that the area behind the settee in the living room serve the same purpose; it became the 'out of sight – out of mind' place to dump things.

Ditto our garden, or in fact both gardens, front and rear. While other families planted these gardens with monkey puzzle trees, with lupines, red hot pokers and wallflowers, and enjoyed making their gardens look attractive, my dad – did absolutely nothing. Both gardens were left to grow wild, and nothing was ever planted in them.

The only time he ever attended to his garden was whenever he received a warning letter from the council. He would then spend a desultory hour or so with a pair of shears before making off to the pub, saying that he was now 'parched' and needed to 'see a man about a dog'.

This little house, number sixty-six Hartington Road, Marden Estate, North Shields was where I spent the next five years of my childhood. Later, as our family increased: Glenda was already with us, four years younger than me, but Marion was just about to come along too, we moved to number forty-four Stanton Road, another newly-built house at the top end of the estate.

That was the place where, after I had passed my eleven plus and I was lucky enough to be able to go to the grammar school; Patricia had come along and was maybe one month old – that was the time that everything fell apart.

Three

Decorators of Taste and Style

'It is really surprising what may be done in the home with a small can of paint, if you aren't careful.' Will Cuppy

A few weeks after we moved in to Hartington Road, I would have been just about four, no older, we painted the gateposts at the front of our houses for our mams and dads. We made a really good job of it too. There was me, Ian Ferguson and Nigel Mackay – and Philip Madison from further down the street decided that his mam and dad would like their gateposts painted too.

I had made the discovery of the paint on one of my scouting missions to the many half-built houses that surrounded us. We often climbed the scaffolding and went in and out of the yet to be completed rooms. Occasionally we would be shouted at by one of the builders, but after they had all finished for the day, the whole of the site was one huge adventure playground. In one way, it was a pity when all the houses were completed: we had to seek our diversions elsewhere.

'Look what I have found,' I said! 'It's paint! We can use this.'

'Where did you find that paint?' Immediate interest from the boys.

'Over there in that house.' The partly finished house over the road, a house that would have some yellow tiles on the facing wall added to it soon – I had seen them - was full of stuff that we could play with. But I believed that our main and most useful purpose was for us to improve the look of our own houses by decorating them with the paint that I had found, and I had managed to bring almost a full can of it from over the road.

We held our very own 'site meeting'. We decided what to do to make our houses look beautiful – and so raise the tone of the neighbourhood.

'If we paint the gates and the gateposts,' said Jimmy, 'our houses will all look the same.' Our houses already did look the same, but that was not the point. Jimmy went on, 'Then everyone will know who is in our gang.'

This, we all agreed, was a brilliant suggestion – and very timely. We had recently begun calling ourselves 'our gang', and this was to differentiate us from Billy Easton down the road and John Thompson up at the top, who also had their gangs. This was the clincher: we all agreed that it was a great idea that everyone who passed by –

particularly Billy Easton and John Thompson – would see where 'our gang' lived.

'And I 've also got brushes.' I said.' There's enough to go round. We can each do a gate and we will get the job done quicker.'

'But we've only got one pot of paint,' said Philip.

'I brought the paint – and I got the brushes, so the paint stays here with me!   That's fair. You'll just have to dip your brush in the paint and run with it.'

The boys agreed, although Philip said that his house was too far away, and he didn't think his mam would like our plan. Philip was a doubter – he always was the last to join in anything, but this time he did have a point. His house was three or four down from us.

'Of course, she'd like our plan,' said Jimmy, completely committed. 'She'll thank us.'

'They'll probably thank us with treats – sweeties and that. Liquorice root's my favourite', said Ian.

'And mine. But it'll be more than sweeties,' said Nigel. I know my mam will want to give us a proper treat – like a reward for our good work. Maybe the Spanish City.'

We all agreed enthusiastically. The Spanish City – city of our dreams. Down in Whitley Bay there was a funfair that all of us had heard about. None of us had been there of course, but we knew people who had – or had said they had been. It was a magical place, a place where you could drive little cars, ride on horses that went round and round; you could get pink candy floss and ice creams for free.

There was a 'Big Dipper' too. The boys who had been to the Spanish City couldn't stop going on about this fantastic ride, but I could not begin to understand what it was, why it existed – but I knew riding on the Big Dipper was going to be my first choice when all our parents took us down there – as now I knew they would.

I was determined to get our project finished quickly, so I set about motivating my team. Ian and Nigel were both on board; Philip needed some persuading.

'I tell you what,' I'd thought this through. 'Philip, you come and help me, and we'll finish my job quicker. Then, I'll bring the paint down to your gate and we can work together on your house.'

The site meeting, including Philip, agreed upon this course of action, and we began our work. I carried the almost-full can of paint and three or four used paint brushes, and I deposited them on that beautiful red pavement in front of my house - next to the gate posts that I was so determined to improve.

The paint that I had obtained turned out to be undercoat. I did not know that at the time, and anyway, it would not have dented my determination in the slightest. It was a sort of greyish-white with red flecks in it and very dull.

I remember its colours very well. (I remembered it for a long time because traces of it on our gate post were there for at least twenty years after the event.) I suppose that if the paint had been stirred properly, it would have mixed into a consistent colour, but when we applied it to the gateposts, first to my house, using the brushes that I had also liberated – one for each of us – the result was very impressive, and it caused us to redouble our efforts.

Having 'finished' our house, we moved on to Philip's, while at the same time Nigel, and then Ian completed the work on their own gateposts. The result was, to the eyes of four four-year-old little boys, quite spectacular. We were more than satisfied with the result: we were delighted.

'Do we do the tops of the posts as well?' was Philip's only question, and it was answered by a loud chorus of expert opinion as we busied ourselves with our work.   The gateposts themselves were quite substantial, made from the same bricks that were used in our houses. Each was maybe eighteen inches square, topped with a raised, dome-like cement finish. My professional opinion was that those tops definitely needed painting, and the site meeting participants all agreed enthusiastically.

And there is no doubt that when we had finished, the gateposts had been made to look so much prettier by every stroke of paint that we had added. Some of the paint spilled on to our lovely red pavement too, but I was quite relaxed about that. At that time, and at that age, I had different ideas of the aesthetic qualities of painted gateposts – as, we soon found out, did all our parents.

We had completed our project, very successfully to, as we thought – it must have taken us about fifteen or twenty minutes – and not one adult had come near us, checked up on us, or even put their head out of one of the four houses that we had 'improved' by our efforts during this time.

So, when Mrs Ferguson did come out of her house, just as we had finished and were admiring our work, the speed at which she rushed down to her own gateposts, the look of amazement and anger that had reddened her face, and the great swipe she took at her son Ian's head with her hand before grabbing him and propelling him towards his front door, came as a bit of a surprise to us.

'Whose idea was this?' Mrs Ferguson stopped and turned to us as she spoke. 'Well? Was it my Ian who suggested this?' Turning to her son who was wiping away his tears as he rubbed his sore head, 'Ian? Was this your idea? What did you think you were doing? You stupid, stupid boy!' Then she looked beyond us at the van that was coming up to a stop outside her gate.

The reason why nobody had been out to see us – except just then for Ian's mam - became clear. Ian's dad, Jimmy Ferguson, had arrived and out from sharing the front bench seat came my mam and Mrs Mackay, Nigel's mother. They had been to the shops, and Jimmy had seen them and brought them home – saving a couple of bus fares.

Jimmy had parked his van by now, but was just standing transfixed, staring in disbelief at what he was seeing. He looked at his gateposts, and his gate, then he looked up and down the street and saw three other sets of 'improved' gate posts and gates.

'Jimmy. Jimmy. Have you seen what these kids have been doing?'

'Bugger! – I'll get some turps.' was all he said. And he was back in his van and off again down to, I suppose, Gladstone's in Cullercoats, as that was probably the nearest hardware shop. In doing so, he left his wife, my mam and Mrs Mackay to cope with what he had obviously decided was a disaster.

They too looked at our decorating work, and instead of being the happy and thankful mams that we expected, Mrs Mackay also burst into tears and my mam came straight for me.

'Anthony Hunt!' These were the first words that my own mam had uttered since arriving. 'Come here!' I moved slowly towards her.

She was looking at our decoration. 'Did you do this?'

'Yes Mam – and Ian and Nigel. Philip helped too....'

'It was Anthony's idea,' said Ian, 'he got the paint and the brushes and everything.'

Nigel chimed in; he had read the new mood, 'Anthony said we should paint all the gates – I didn't want to do it, Mam. I tried to stop him!'

The lying little sod. Until that moment, I thought of him as my main ally. He was enthusiastic, as enthusiastic as me, but here he was betraying our friendship by snitching about me.

I remember this incident particularly well because I think it affected our subsequent relationship. As kids, we continued to play together until I moved to Stanton Road. We were in the same class at school for a long time, then Alan Gibson and I were pushed up a couple of years at Cullercoats Junior.

We finished year three at Cullercoats, and then moved to the new Monkhouse Primary School on Marden Estate – but we began the next school year in year two as the first intake ever at that school. So, I had lost contact with Nigel at school until we met again at the High school when we were eleven.

By then the friendship had ended, and although we were both in the cubs and scouts together, we lived in a kind of parallel universe. The last time our separate existences came together was when we fought each other while we were at scout camp up in Northumberland. And after that, we never spoke to each other again.

Telling on me, 'snitching' to his mam, didn't save Nigel from a clout round the head, followed by the imperious command to go to his room and wait for the return of his father.

I got 'walloped' – that was my dad's term – on his return from work that night. Earlier I had also had the 'Bring me that hairbrush!' treatment from my mam. Over the knees, half a dozen painful blows on my bare bum, delivered from the hard, blue back of my mother's special Mason Pearson hairbrush. I wonder if that hairbrush was designed as a dual-purpose implement?

As I remember it, it was a better weapon than it was a hairbrush. The bristles seemed to scratch my young scalp rather than brush it, so I avoided it whenever I could, and the weight and balance of it meant that my mother used it as her weapon of choice on my, and sometimes on my sisters' backsides, until I was too big to be prepared to submit to the indignity.

All of the 'decorators' were punished according to the disciplinary procedures of the four families involved. I came out of it particularly badly, as I was not only punished twice, 'hair brushed' by my mam, 'walloped' by my dad, but my dad also compounded things by exiling me to my room and telling me that I would stay there until I 'learned to behave'.

Twenty or more years later, I could still see the remains of our paintwork on one of the gateposts, and I bet that if we went to look now, traces of the great painting project of our gang would still be there, as try as they might, the parents could not get rid of all traces – our work came with a guarantee. It is just that the quality service we had provided was not appreciated by the customer.

Four
Liquorice Root

'Opportunity makes a thief' Francis Bacon

My Junior school is in John Street, Cullercoats. This is my third year at this school – I was in the infants for two years, and now I am in Year One in the juniors. My teacher is Mrs Ross. I started in the Infants, and Reg Carr, a boy who is a year older than me, took me there for my first day at school. He used to walk to school with me every day, as he lives just two doors up from us on Hartington Road, but he doesn't take me to school now. I think he got bored, so sometimes I go with Ian or Nigel, but I often just go by myself.

It's quite a long walk to Cullercoats, over the Broadway which is a main road, and sometimes over the railway bridge at the station – if I try to take the short cut. Although my mam says she is a housewife now and she stays at home – she doesn't go out to work, she never takes me to school – or meets me at school at three o'clock when the bell goes. She does 'housework' and that means that she works in the house, I suppose, so she can't take me to school or bring me back.

Every day we have dinner in the school dining room. We all walk across the road in a crocodile and we sit at our tables. The ladies then give us our dinners. My mam says that because I have a school dinner, I don't need to have a big breakfast, so I am always hungry when the bell goes for dinner at school. Mam can have a little rest in bed when I get dressed, and I give her a kiss and leave the house while she lights her cigarette and takes her cup of coffee back to bed.

Last week in our school assembly, Mr Wightman our headmaster, told us that many children are catching a disease called 'polio', and that we all must have an injection to keep us safe. We are to tell our parents. I tell this to my mam: she says I won't be able to have the injection because I have asthma and eczema, and I might have a 'reaction'. My mam used to be a nurse; she knows these things.

When I go to school the next day, I tell Mrs Ross that my mam said I can't have the injection. She writes something down in her book. I ask her what 'polio' is. She says that it is a germ that is in the air. You can't see it, but it is there, and sometimes we breathe it in through mouths and our noses. And the injection? The injection is like wearing a suit of armour and the polio can't hurt us then. I am worried about catching polio, and if I don't have the injection, will the polio come looking for me?

Today I decide that if I can't have the injection, I will stop the polio from catching me. On my way to school this morning, I zig zag all the way. Sometimes I run and then suddenly I stop. I pretend to turn to one side, and then I turn to the other side. It seems to work – I don't think the polio can catch me if I move quickly.

I hold my hand over my face so that I don't breathe the polio in through my mouth and nose. I will do this when I am outside from now on. Maybe I will try to make a mask to cover my nose and mouth: I think that will help.

My Uncle Tom came to our house yesterday. He was having a cup of tea with my mam when I got home from school. Uncle Tom is a sailor, and he only comes home for a short time, and then he goes away again. He has been to Japan before and this time his ship went to Canada.

He has brought us some presents, and one of the presents he brought for me is a case of Carnation Milk. Forty-eight tins, he says to my mam. This is to help me with my eczema. I am not happy with this present because I have had Carnation Milk before, and I hate it.

But the other presents he has for me make up for the Carnation Milk. He's brought me a brand-new pair of blue jeans with silver studs on the pockets, and a red and white checked shirt.

Uncle Tom tells me that all little Canadian boys wear these jeans, and that my new shirt is the best shirt for cowboys to wear. He's also brought me a belt for my jeans; it's made with real leather and it has patterns and little coloured beads on it. Then he says that if I want, I can be a real cowboy, and he opens another bag and takes out a box.

He gives it to me to open. It's a gun – a real cowboy's pistol. It is a shiny golden colour, and it has a beautiful white handle. It's not a real gun, of course, but it looks real. He tells me that it is a 'revolver' – the kind of gun all cowboys use – and when you pull the trigger, you can see the bullets moving around. So, I pull the trigger, and it makes a noise like a real gun. My mam says it is far too loud and I mustn't fire it in the house.

Uncle Tom has brought me this gun because he knows I like Roy Rogers. Roy Rogers was my hero. I have one of his books, 'The Roy Rogers Cowboy Annual – UK Edition', and it has a picture of Trigger on the cover. His white horse is called Trigger; Roy Rogers' wife is called Dale Evans, not Dale Rogers, and she has a horse as well. When Uncle Tom went to sea last time, he asked me what I would like as a present when he came back. I told him that I wanted to look like Roy Rogers. And he remembered. I had forgotten all of this because it was a long time ago, and it is a surprise that he has come to my house specially to see me and to give me my Roy Rogers presents.

I don't tell him that Davey Crockett is my hero now. I really want one of those Davey Crockett hats; Reg Carr has one and he wears it to go to school, but when I mention this to Mam, she shushes me and tells me to be polite.

The best present of all is the last parcel that he takes out of his bag. He has brought me something he calls a 'jerkin'. Whatever he calls it, it is just fantastic – I want to put it on straight away, and I never want to take it off. Mam looks at it, then rubs the material with her fingers. She says it is made of satin.

My new jerkin is blue, bright blue, with a red lining and a zipper that goes right up to my chin. There are two pockets for my hands and two other pockets on my chest. These pockets fasten with silver buttons, and when I put it on and we fasten the zipper up, my mam and Uncle Tom are very pleased. Mam says it is exactly the right size, although, it's not - it is much too big for me and I say so, but they say I look perfect – 'a real Roy Rogers', as Uncle Tom says, although I would have preferred to be Davey Crockett.

Uncle Tom says that if I wear my new jerkin when I go to school, I will be 'the bee's knees' and all the other boys will be jealous. I think that is a great idea, and I ask my mam if I can wear it tomorrow. Mam gives Uncle Tom a funny look and then she says, of course not, the jerkin is for 'best'. But Uncle Tom whispers something in her ear and she looks at him again, and then at me and says yes, all right then, I can wear my new jerkin when I go to school tomorrow.

So, this morning I am on my way to school – and I am wearing my new jerkin – not my new jeans or my new shirt because mam would not let me wear all my new things, but she has kept her promise about the jerkin. I go down the road to school, dodging the polio, and I know that I look just like a little Canadian boy would look on his way to school.

Today is Friday. Every Friday when I go to school, I take my dinner money with me. When I started school, a week's school dinners cost two and eleven pence. They now cost three and sixpence. (Later they would cost four and tuppence, and when I left Cullercoats school, they cost five shillings per week.)

I have put the money for my school dinners in one of the top pockets of my new jerkin, and I have fastened the silver button to keep the money safe.

When I get to school, everybody likes my new jerkin, and even some of the girls want to touch it because somebody says it is made of satin. Mrs Ross then calls the register and asks us for our dinner money.

When I go to the teacher's desk to pay for next week's dinners, I undo the pocket of my jerkin and take out the coins. Something is wrong – when my mam gave me my dinner money this morning, she gave me three coins: a two-shilling piece, a one shilling piece and a sixpence.

I can't find the sixpence. I tell Mrs Ross that I can't find the sixpence; I have lost it. She also looks in my pockets, all of them, but the sixpence is not there. She tells me that I can bring the missing sixpence on Monday, and that I must tell my mam what has happened, and I go back to my desk and sit down.

I've just found the sixpence! It was in my pocket – just where I put it, but it slipped down right into the corner.

I want to tell Mrs Ross that I've found the sixpence, but Mr Wightman has come into our classroom and she is talking to him. They are looking towards me. Have I done something wrong? Will she be angry if I tell her that I have found the money? I better wait and give it to my mam. She will understand.

We have been doing some group reading this morning. Usually I love reading – it is my favourite time, but today I keep thinking about the sixpence. I worry that it is there in my jerkin, in my pocket. Nobody can see it, but I know it is there. I feel that I have done something naughty, but I don't think that Mrs Ross will be happy if I find the money and then give it to her. She finished collecting the dinner money a long time ago, and she's already sent a monitor with the tin and the class register to the office like she does every week.

I am going to keep the money in my pocket. It is better if I pretend I have lost it. I don't want to get into trouble with Mrs Ross.

I can't take the money home because my mam will be cross with me, so I have decided what I will do.

When the bell rings, I don't join the crocodile, but I wait by the pegs until everyone has gone across the road for dinner. I walk down John Street towards the sea, and I go in to the sweet shop on the corner and I buy three sticks of liquorice root. They cost two pennies each, so that's the sixpence spent. It won't be in my pocket, worrying me, this afternoon.

I chew on one straight away, and don't really want to chew another, so I offer one of my sticks to Marion Thompson when I get back to school. I like Marion Thompson, she is in my class, but she is six months older than me. (I like Marion Thompson so much, that I now have a sister called Marion!)

Marion Thompson says she hates liquorice root, and she doesn't want anything at all from me - ever. I don't want to start chewing on another stick now – I'm not sure how much I like liquorice root. Not as much as I thought – and I am a bit hungry now. I've only had a small bottle of milk at break time, Mam hadn't time to make me any breakfast. I wish I had joined the crocodile.

I now have two sticks of liquorice root left, but I can't take them in to school because Mrs Ross will want to know how I got them. I have hidden them on the high shelf in the boys' toilet, and I will collect them before I leave, and I will eat them on my way home tonight.

This afternoon is 'painting'. We are 'taking the line for a walk'. You paint a squiggly line in black paint on to a sheet of sugar paper. You make a lot of loops and circles. Then you colour in the loops and circles and it makes a painting.

Marion Thompson has left her painting and has just gone up to Mrs Ross's desk. She and Mrs Ross are talking together, and then they both look at me. Mrs Ross writes something on a piece of paper and folds it in two. She gives Marion the piece of paper and she goes out of the classroom holding it in that special way that monitors hold things when they take messages.

I have just spilled some paint. Some of the paint splashes on me and I try to wipe it off with my painting cloth, but it just smudges. I should have taken off my jerkin – or put on one of the painting pinnies, but I forgot. I hope that I can make my jerkin clean or my mam will be very angry with me.

Marion Thompson has just come back in to the classroom. She says something to Mrs Ross. They both look at me. Ian Ferguson has just said that my face is very red. He laughs.

Mr Wightman wants to see me, and Mrs Ross says I must go straight to his office now.

It is about the sixpence. Mr Wightman asks me why did I keep the sixpence and why I did not give it to Mrs Ross this morning. I say that I lost it, and I don't know what happened to it.

Mr Wightman says that he knows what happened to it. How does he know? I haven't told anybody. I haven't spoken to anyone – except

Marion Thompson. Oh. Marion Thompson. She told Mrs Ross, and Marion took a note to Mr Wightman.

Mr Wightman says that I am thief. I say that I am not, and he tells me to be quiet. He says I am a thief, and do I know what happens to thieves? I say no, I don't know – and I say I am not a thief. I found the sixpence later and I didn't know what to do.

He doesn't want to hear me. He tells me to stop making excuses. What happens to thieves, he says, is that they get punished. He then tells me to hold out my hand.

Mr Wightman picks up his cane from the desk and, holding my wrist with his left hand, he hits me on the palm of my hand with his cane. He hits me three times. He then takes the other hand and hits me again another three times.

Both my hands are hurting, and I have started to cry.

Mr Wightman says this is what happens to thieves, and that he has caned me six times – one time for every penny that I stole. If I steal anything again, ever, Mr Wightman says he won't cane me. He will call a policeman and I will go to prison.

I must go home now, he says, because he does not want a thief in his school. If I am to return to school on Monday, I must return as a 'good boy, not as a 'nasty little thief'. Can I do that?

I say that yes, I can, and Mr Wightman says good, but that he does not want me to go back to the classroom today. He will tell Mrs Ross what has happened, and that he is sending me straight home now.

He says that he is also going to write a letter to my parents and I must wait outside his door while he writes it.

I have stopped crying now, and I am walking back up Mast Lane on my way home. I am not dodging the polio any more. I am carrying an envelope with a letter from Mr Wightman in it. I could say that I lost it if anybody asks me. Do you think anybody will ask?

And anyway, it's my new jerkin that now worries me more than anything. It's got a big black mark on it, and I know my mam is going to be mad.

Five
Dorothy Sykes

'We didn't realise we were making memories, we just thought we were having fun.' AA Milne

Dorothy Sykes is six years old. She is one year older than me and she lives next door at number sixty-eight. She is the only girl who I ever play with. Her mother is called Madge and her dad is called Louis. Auntie Madge is funny to look at. She is very fat, with a big belly, but she has the thinnest legs you have ever seen. She's like a big round ball with matchsticks for her legs.

Dorothy's dad, Louis, is a sailor and he is away at sea almost all the time. I have only ever seen him once; he has huge bushy eyebrows, but he is very friendly, and Dorothy talks about him all the time.

Her grandad is called Lionel, and he also lives at number sixty-eight. He likes gardening and has special tools. He planted a monkey puzzle tree in the middle of the front garden, and he cut a circle in the lawn around it. One of his special tools allows him to make an edge around that circle. In the borders of Dorothy's front lawn, he has planted some flowers and he often shows Dorothy and me what he has just planted, and he likes to tell us what the new flowers are called. I remember wallflowers and lupins, but not the others. Oh yes, red hot pokers, I remember them too.

He is very proud of his garden, and he tells Dorothy and me that he loves gardening. He likes things to look neat and tidy. I do too. The last time he told me that he likes things to be neat and tidy, I noticed that he looked over towards our front garden.

Our garden is not neat and tidy: it is a mess. Even I know that. The grass is long, there are bits of wood, bricks and smelly stuff hidden in the long, straggly grass, and my mam says that I will hurt myself if I trip over something, so I mustn't play there.

I wish my dad had some tools like Dorothy's Grandad Lionel, but he has told my mam that he hates gardening and anyway, he hasn't got any time – he already has three jobs; how many more does she want him to have?

Mam does not like gardens either, and she won't do any gardening 'not for all the tea in China'. That is not her job. She is a housewife. She likes to smoke her cigarettes and drink coffee with Auntie Madge, her best friend. And Mam is going to have a baby soon.

She tells me that I am going to have a new baby brother or a sister. She doesn't know if it will be a boy or a girl, but she knows that I will be very useful around the house when the new baby comes because Glenda is too young to help. She also says you can't have a baby and do the gardening, and Auntie Madge agrees.

Grandad Lionel has offered to look after our garden, and he came round to our house last night when Dad came home from work. He said that he was happy to cut the grass and plant some pretty flowers, but would my dad tidy it up first. My dad was quite angry; he said that he doesn't want anybody working in his garden, and he told Grandad Lionel to mind his own business and go back to his own house.

I was surprised: Grandad Lionel is a very friendly man, and I think that my mam was upset by what my dad said. She said to my dad that Grandad Lionel was only offering to help, but my dad said that he had 'no time to sit here and argue the toss with busybodies' as he had to go off to work again.

He plays the piano in Whitley Bay in the evenings, so he only comes home to change his clothes and then he goes out straight away. I think I must have been asleep when he came home last night, and again when he went off to work this morning because I didn't see him.

My mam was worried about Grandad Lionel, and last night, after my dad went to work, she left me to listen out for Glenda while she went to have a cup of coffee with Auntie Madge.

***

Today is Saturday and we do not go to school, and when I knock on Dorothy's door, Auntie Madge says that Grandad Lionel is not very well. She says that he needs to rest, and Dorothy and I must play quietly so that we do not disturb him.

'We'll play out,' says Dorothy to me. 'We'll go up the road and see if there are any children playing in the field.'

At the top of the road, there is a big field where all the children like to meet. There is a lot of building going on there, new houses everywhere. Some shops are being built, with houses and flats above them, but there are still lots of places where we can play.

I like playing there because we can find our chewing gum, and I like that. We call it 'tarrie toosh', and the builders leave large strips of it lying about when they stop working. I see it in the new buildings: they sometimes lay it between rows of bricks, but we like to tear off little pieces of it, then we chew it. It is just like chewing gum, but we don't swallow it, we spit it out.

Auntie Madge thinks that it is a good idea if we play out, but she says that we mustn't play in any of the new buildings as we might hurt ourselves. She asks me if my mam thinks it's all right if we play out. I run back in and shout up the stairs to ask her.

My mam is still in bed – she has her coffee and her cigarette now while Glenda plays in her playpen. I think that my dad must be out delivering the milk for Jimmy Ferguson because I have not seen him today.

Mam says that she is on her way down, give her a moment because she wants to have a word with Auntie Madge. She comes to the back door.

'Mac, these children want to go out to play. Is that all right with you? It would make things easier for me today.' My mam is always called 'Mac' although her real name is Agnes. When she was a little girl, her mam and dad always made her carry her mackintosh with her wherever she went.

'What's the matter Madge? Is Lionel all right?'

'Oh, he'll be fine. I think it would be better if the children played out for a while.' She then says something silently to Mam – her lips move, but no sound comes out, and I don't understand what she is saying.

Mam says, 'Oh. All right. Yes, of course. Good idea.' And then to Dorothy and me she says, 'Mind you two don't get up to any mischief. And promise you won't play on any of the buildings.'

We promise to be good, and Mam gives me a kiss.

Auntie Madge does not give Dorothy a kiss, but she tells my mam that she is going to Mrs Mackay's now because she wants to make a telephone call, and then to us she says that we can go out now, but we must come back home for our dinners.

I follow Dorothy as we run on to the grass to walk up to the field. Across the road from where we live, there is a wide strip of grass that goes all the way up to the field where we will play.

We are going to walk up to the top of the road, but we decide to stop and sit on the wall outside Mrs Jackson's house because she is playing her music. She always plays very loud music on her record player and she sings along with it. Her voice is very loud as well, and my dad says she could have been an opera singer.

We can sometimes hear her singing in my house, the music is so loud, and mam tells me it is 'that American country' music, but that she is a 'common' person and that is the kind of music that 'common' people like.

Mrs Jackson has two favourite country music singers, and she plays their records all the time. They are Slim Whitman and Hank Williams. She has told us – the last time that we sat on her wall – that she knows all the words to all the songs. We listen to her singing for a few minutes. She can sing very well, but she makes a lot of noise, and I am sure that most of the street can hear her singing.

Dorothy is sitting next to me and she says that Auntie Madge is going to telephone the doctor because Grandad Lionel is not very well. He is in bed now, but last night, Dorothy tells me that he was crying. I have never seen a man cry before – I thought that only babies cry – that's what my dad says when I cry, anyway. I hope that the doctor will make Grandad Lionel better because I like him.

Brian Jackson comes out to see us. He is Mrs Jackson's son and he is the same age as me. We don't play with Brian because his mam never lets him. The other boys tease him because there is something wrong with Brian. He is always unhappy, and it is very easy to make him cry.

We say that we are going up to play on the field, but then Mrs Jackson puts her head out of the window and calls Brian in. She is a very pretty woman, but there is no Mr Jackson. I have never seen Brian's dad.

Dorothy and I walk up the road. We are going to see if there are any other children up there. If there are not, we will get some tarrie toosh and bring it back home to chew. We often chew our tarrie toosh in our wash house because we can hide it there, and nobody ever looks for it.

Dorothy's wash house has been painted white by Grandad Lionel, and Auntie Madge does all her washing in it. Our wash house is full of old things, and there is no room in it, but it is a good hiding place, and both Dorothy and I use it to hide our secret things.

There is a great big field at the top of our road, but today we see that there are no children playing on it. We turn the corner on to Honister Road, thinking about walking down the row of 'self-builds' behind our houses so that we can complete the circle and get back home, but we come across some men working on the pavement in front of us.

There is a small tent on the pavement, and there are some men standing around a big hole in the ground, and they have covered this hole with the tent. As they move from their lorry to the tent, we can see the hole in the ground as one side of the tent is wide open.

The men are busy fixing lots of wires and pipes in the hole, but one of them looks up, smiles and says hello. He asks what we are doing, and Dorothy says that we've come up to the field to play.

The man says would we like a cup of tea, and as he asks us, another man turns to look at us and he smiles too.

'Put the kettle on, John,' he says, 'We have some guests for tea.' John looks at us and says, 'Yes, you've come at a good time. Tea break. You two sit down and I'll get the tea ready. Do you like biscuits?'

Dorothy and I are to be the guests. She and I sit down on the wall, and the man asks our names while John sets light to a small stove, on which he places the kettle.

As the kettle boils, the man gets five cups and puts them down on the wall next to us. He then says, 'Oh yes. You haven't met – I have got a surprise for you!' I don't know what he means, but I have no time to wonder because at that moment he says to someone in the tent, someone we haven't seen, 'Maurice! Come and meet our guests.' He then smiles at us again.

A man who must have been working in the hole with the pipes and wires comes out of the tent and he says hello to the both of us.

He is a black man. And he is tall, very tall: he has a lovely warm smile, but his skin is a deep, deep brown colour. Dorothy and I have never seen a man with this colour skin before, and his face is different too. He has a flat nose and big lips, and when he speaks to us, he speaks in English – I can understand what he is saying – but he says the words in a way I have never heard before.

In the very sensitive times in which I am writing this account, I have worried over how to describe this man. I am aware that any descriptor of any kind that alludes to race, to colour or ethnicity can be pounced upon by a reader looking for inappropriate inferences, looking to take offence. But this man was the first 'black' man I had ever seen, and his strong West Indian accent added to the sense of confusion – and wonder – that Dorothy and I experienced.

When I tell you that he then proceeded to sing us a calypso, a calypso that included references to England, Jamaica, North Shields, to 'Dorothy' and 'Anthony' – yes, we were in his song too – your credulity may well be stretched. But it did happen. This man sat with us and while we all enjoyed a cup of tea together - and biscuits, he told us of the island where he came from, the family that he had left behind, the boat that had brought him to England, and the new job that he had just started that week.

He was happy to be in England, happy to have a job, and happy to sing his calypso to two little kids without any trace of irony or any thought at all that he was being patronised by his colleagues. It was a genuinely innocent moment.

I appreciate that moment now more than I did then, of course. The cup of tea and the biscuit – and being treated as the 'guests' of these men – they were real high points of that short interlude.

We finish our cup of tea, and the men say that they must get back to work. Dorothy and I continue our walk, looking for something to do, someone to play with, but can't see anyone at all.

When we arrive back home, we see that Mam and Auntie Madge are sitting outside having a cup of coffee. They often do this. Each brings a kitchen chair outside and as usual, they are both smoking their cigarettes.

'Hello pets,' says Auntie Madge, 'You are back quickly.'

'We've had a cup of tea with some men,' says Dorothy, 'and they gave us a biscuit.'

'One of them was a black man,' I add. 'He sang a song for us and we sat down and listened to it. Then the men went back to work, and we walked down the back and came home.'

'Who were these men?' My mam looks serious and she looks at Auntie Madge.

'They were workmen up the road,' says Dorothy, 'They had a tent over a big hole in the pavement, and when they had their tea break, they gave us a cup of tea.'

'And we had biscuits.' I add. The biscuits are important.

Mam smiles and lights another cigarette. She taps her feet to the sound of the music from across the road. Mrs Jackson is still singing.

'Your Stan says that she is very talented,' says Auntie Madge. 'She's got a lovely voice.' And she smiles as she taps the ash away from her cigarette.

My mam looks at her. 'When did Stan say that?'

'What do you mean?'

'When did Stan say she was talented? When did he say she had a lovely voice?' My mam looks at Auntie Madge in a special way, and Auntie Madge stops smiling.

'Oh, I don't know, Mac. She does have a lovely voice. He just made a comment. I don't know when he said it.'

Mam says, 'He said it to you?'

'No, it was a while ago. Maybe the last time Louis was here? Yes, he told Louis and Louis told me.'

I wish my mam would ask me. I could tell her. Mrs Jackson came over here one day last week and dad played the piano while she sang. Then she sat down and had a cup of coffee and a cigarette with Dad.

Mam was out. She had gone to see my grandma and dad stayed at home to look after me and Glenda that day. He sent me out to play. If she asks me, I will tell her, but she doesn't. Instead, Auntie Madge looks towards Dorothy and me.

'You two – you must be starving. I 'll tell you what – I've got some sandwich spread in my cupboard and some lovely bread. I'll make you something to eat before Christine comes over.' She stubs out her cigarette.

'Why is Christine coming over, Mam?' Dorothy asks.

I like Christine. She is Stephen Robson's big sister, she's very old, I think she's fifteen, and she lives across the road, and she is always very friendly to me.

'She's going to the beach this afternoon – down to Cullercoats Bay. And she said that she wants to take you two with her.'

Dorothy jumps up and down; she is delighted, 'Can I go swimming too, Mam? With Christine?' She holds both her mam's hands as she jumps up and down, saying, 'Please Mam – please Mam – please Mam.' Her mam says, 'All right then, but be careful and promise to stay where Christine can see you.' Dorothy says of course she will, and then she says to me that she's going to go in and get her swimming costume.

Auntie Madge says she will help Dorothy to look, and she tells my mam to send me over the wall for my dinner – for my sandwich spread.

Mam says she will, and she says thank you to Auntie Madge. Then she says to me, 'Anthony, do you know where your swimming trunks are? I'll go and get them for you while you have something to eat with Dorothy.'

'No Mam, I haven't seen them for ages.'

'You had them on when you played with Ian and Philip last week.'

'I haven't seen them, mam. I don't know where they are.'

'I'll go in and have a look for them now. I'll see if I can find them. Go over to Dorothy's and have something to eat. When I find them, I'll throw them over – and you will need a towel.'

She won't find my swimming trunks, I know that! I do have some, but I have hidden them in the wash house. My mam won't find them and even if she does, I won't ever wear them again.

It was on that really hot day last week, and my mam said that she was going out and I had to go and play in Ian Ferguson's back garden.

Ian was wearing his swimming trunks, and so was Philip Madison. The boys were playing with water, so Mam made me wear my trunks as well. My swimming trunks are horrible: they are made of wool and they are very itchy, but even worse, as soon as they get wet, they get very heavy and they start to stretch – right down to my knees.

When this happened last week, the boys laughed at me, and Mrs Ferguson was also laughing, I think. So, I'm not going to wear them again - ever, and that is why I have hidden them somewhere my mam never looks – in the wash house.

But if we are going to the beach this afternoon, something else worries me even more. I do want to go with Christine, and I do like the beach. It is very close to my school and I see the sea every day on my way there. If I walk a little further down the road from my school and look over the railings, I can see Cullercoats Bay, so I know where we are going.

But I can't swim! My mam knows that. She has always told me to keep away from the sea – and never, ever to go on to the beach. Dorothy has told me she has been to the open-air swimming pool in Tynemouth and to the baths at Hawkeys Lane, and that she can almost swim. I know that Christine is a good swimmer: she is almost grown up, and she often goes swimming. But I can't swim, I have never even been to a swimming pool – and I dare not go in the sea.

It is because of my skin – my eczema. It's on the back of my legs and the inside of my elbows now, and my fingers and toes too are all dry and sore. I won't be able to go in the sea because the salt water will hurt me too much. My mam knows this, but she wants me to go swimming with Christine and Dorothy. I don't understand why.

Auntie Madge has made us our lunch. She has buttered a slice of bread for each of us and has put some sandwich spread on each slice. Then she has cut each slice of bread in half. We also have half an apple and a glass of milk and water to 'wash it down'.

'Is Grandad Lionel better now?' I ask Dorothy. 'Has the doctor been to see him?'

Auntie Madge answers, 'Yes pet, he is much better. The doctor has given him some medicine and says that he will soon be up and about again. But today he must rest, so Christine will take you down to Cullercoats Bay.'

The way down to Cullercoats Bay is exactly the same way that I go to school every day. Dorothy goes to Cullercoats Junior school also, but we never go together. She goes to school with another girl, John Thompson's sister, Marion, but Marion does not like me.

So today is strange. On my way to school, I often turn into Silloth Place – Reg Carr took me that way once – but Dorothy says she has never been that way. Christine says that is the way she often goes too, so today we walk through Silloth Place before we walk over the Broadway and down Mast Lane.

As we cross the railway bridge, we see the sea. Both Dorothy and I see it every morning, but usually we take no notice. Today is different: and we carry on past our school on the right, and down to Cullercoats village.

Just past the aquarium we go down the ramp to the sand. I am pleased that we are not going to the aquarium – I have been there twice, and it is a very smelly place – but today Christine takes us to the 'Fairy Cave'.

There are two caves on the beach that some people say are smugglers' caves, Christine tells us, but really, they are Fairy caves and if we are lucky, we might see a fairy. I don't know anything about smugglers, but I know that I have never seen a fairy before, so I rush on to the first cave hoping to see one. Christine says that I might frighten the fairies if I make a noise, so I slow down and sneak towards the cave.

I don't see any fairies, but Christine says that she is going in to the cave to get changed into her swimming costume and she will see if she can see any and will let me know. Dorothy also goes in to the cave to get changed, but I don't. I don't have a swimming costume – my mam couldn't find it ha-ha – so I am to 'play on the beach and stay near the girls and not get into trouble'.

I am quite happy because that means that I don't have to get my skin wet, and the salt water can't hurt me.

Christine and Dorothy come out of the cave and run towards the water. Christine is very tall, and I think that she is beautiful, and she looks like a princess in her blue and white swimsuit. Dorothy is quite fat: she has thin legs and ankles like her mam and she doesn't look like a princess, but she is laughing as she runs into the waves.

They both scream a little when they get to the sea because the water is so cold, but Christine dives in and starts swimming straight away. Dorothy stays by the shoreline, so I can go and talk to her, although I keep well away from the water.

'Are you not going to go in?' I ask Dorothy. 'Christine is good at swimming, isn't she?'

'Yes, but she is much older than me. I can swim – a little, but only in the swimming pool, not in the sea.'

'Why?'

Dorothy tries to explain, 'The swimming pool is like a big bath, and I can float in it. Also, my mam holds me up.' I try to imagine Auntie Madge in a swimming pool with her big round body and her skinny little legs, but I can't. I ask, 'Can you swim here, in the sea, like Christine?'

'I can,' says Dorothy, 'but I won't. Not today.' She sits down next to me on the sand. She looks sad.

'Why? What's wrong?'

'Mummy says my grandad is very poorly. He can't get out of bed.'

'But Auntie Madge said that the doctor has given him some medicine.'

'Yes, I know. But what if the medicine hasn't worked? My mam told your mam that as soon as we were off to the beach, she was going back round to Mrs Mackay's.'

'To make a telephone call?'

'Yes, to call the doctor again.'

Dorothy and I sit together and don't speak. I think that we are thinking about the same thing. I know that I am thinking about Grandad Lionel, and I imagine that she is too, but I don't ask.

Christine swims back to us. She stands up in the water and walks towards us, 'Are you not coming in, Dorothy?' she says as she shakes water out of her hair, 'Once you get in it's not cold at all. If you like, I'll take you in and hold you while you practise your swimming, just like your mam does.'

I am hoping that Dorothy will say yes to that. I want to know if she really can swim, or if she is telling fibs. But she shakes her head and says, 'No, it's all right, thank you. I don't want to go swimming today.'

'But while we are here, and I am already wet – it would be a good idea to try. Come on, come and have a swim with me,' and she tries to take Dorothy's hand.

Dorothy snatches her hand away and says no thank you, she wants to go back home to see her mummy. Christine looks at her but doesn't ask again.

I wish I could go swimming with Christine. I wish that she would take my hand and lead me into the water where she could hold me up, and I could get closer to her. She is very beautiful.

Christine walks past us and says, 'All right then, in that case, we better get ourselves changed,' and she walks back up to the Fairy Cave.

Dorothy gets up to follow her and I say, 'Do you think she is angry?' Dorothy shrugs her shoulders and gets up to follow Christine. When we get to the entrance to the cave I hear Christine say, 'Anthony, you stay there please. Dorothy and I are going to get changed now.'

I know they are! Of course, I#I know they are – and I want to see! I don't want to see Dorothy, but I do want to see Christine. I want to look at her as she puts her clothes on.

Slowly I creep in to the fairy cave as far as I can; they are both there, and I can see shadows of people moving. And I think that Christine is nearer, and Dorothy is further in, so I inch a little way forward.

She sees me. 'Anthony Hunt! What are you doing, you naughty boy?' I think that she is laughing because she does not sound angry.

'Nothing, I was just seeing if you were all right – I was looking for the fairies.'

'There are none here, and we don't want little boys spying on us, do we Dorothy?'

I don't hear what Dorothy says, but I know what it will be.

I walk back to the entrance to the cave to wait. There is another cave very close by, and I move over there, very slowly, to see if there are fairies there. Maybe that is the fairy cave, not this one. I don't want to frighten them away, but even when I walk very slowly, I don't see any.

Christine and Dorothy come out of the cave. Christine sees me and smiles, 'You are a naughty boy, Anthony. Ladies like to have some privacy when they get changed. Don't we, Dorothy?'

Dorothy nods and then says, 'Can we go home now please?'

'Of course,' says Christine. 'We'll go to the top of the ramp and there we will wipe our feet properly. We don't want to walk home with sand in our shoes, as it will make our feet sore.'

This we do. Christine wipes her feet first, but then she wipes Dorothy's feet very carefully as well.

She asks me if I want her to wipe my feet, and I say no thanks. I would love her to wipe them in the same way that she has wiped Dorothy's, but I don't want her to see the eczema on them. I have kept my shoes and socks on anyway, so I think that my feet will be all right.

Halfway back up the road, I realise that I have got sand in my shoes, and that my feet are scratchy and sore. I must put some of my special cream on them when I get home.

As we arrive back at Hartington Road, Christine goes in to see Auntie Madge to tell her that we are back home. Auntie Madge comes out to see us. She is crying. My mam is with her and she is crying too.

Auntie Madge whispers something to Christine, who nods. She then says that she had better get home now, but if there is anything she or her mam can do, Auntie Madge has only to ask. Auntie Madge says thank you.

Christine waves goodbye to Dorothy and me; she is sad now as well, and she walks across the road to her house. Auntie Madge turns to Dorothy, takes hold of her and gives her a cuddle.

My mam says that she had better get home to put the tea on, and she takes me by the hand. Because she has come out of Auntie Madge's front door, we walk back to our house by going out of Dorothy's gate and into my gate – instead of hopping over as we normally do.

Mam tells me that Grandad Lionel has gone away now, and he won't be coming back. I hope he does come back because he is a very kind man, and I like him.

Six
Jamboree

'Education is important, but camping is importanter' Anon

'I have received a letter from the Chief Scout today,' says Mr Carr, our Akela, 'He has invited our wolf cub pack to a 'Jamboree'.' Reg Carr lives about three doors up from us on Hartington Road. His son, also called Reg, took me to school on my first day. I sometimes go to school with him, but not very often because he is two years older than me.

'Akela', as I must call Mr Carr when I am at cubs, is the man who suggested to my mam that I join the cub pack. I went along and watched on the first night and I really liked it. The boys all sit around in a circle, and Akela gives them some orders. Then they all chant some promises together and they go into their sixes.

A 'six' is a group of up to six boys who work together as a team. They have a 'Sixer' and a 'Seconder' who are the bosses of the team. Akela then sets a task for the six, and the six that performs the task the best, scores some points on the Roll of Honour.

There are other things that we do as well. We can earn badges by learning how to perform certain tasks: being an Observer, an Artist, a Book Reader, a Camper or a First Aider. Each badge you get is sewn on to your cub shirt by your mam, and if you get some special badges, you can get a 'Leaping Wolf' badge to wear on your chest.

I would love to have the leaping wolf badge on my cub uniform, but it is hard as you have to do so many tasks. You must be able to light a fire, cook some meat on the fire, make a shelter outside and sleep in it overnight – these are all tasks in the Outdoorsman badge. I also must become a First Aider, as well as doing something called a 'Personal Challenge', and I have no idea what that means.

I must also keep a log book; that is like a diary, and I must make a record of all the things I do for my personal challenge. I think that I am going to need some help here. You can see that the leaping wolf badge is a really difficult challenge, Reg Carr already has it: he said it was easy. I am not so sure.

I like the idea of collecting badges on my cub uniform, but when I first got my new cub jumper, it was very uncomfortable for me to wear. It is made of green wool, and it is very itchy. My mam found a long-sleeved vest for me to wear under it, so that I don't get too itchy. That seems to work quite well, and I am not scratching as much now.

I also have to wear a green cap with thin yellow stripes, a neckerchief with a leather woggle, and long grey socks with green 'garter tabs'. Mam said that she paid a lot of money for this uniform, so she hopes that I will keep my promise. (I promised that if she bought me the uniform, I would stay in the cubs and not leave.)

Akela says that cubs must always be smartly dressed, and at the beginning of each pack meeting, we have an inspection. Akela chooses a different sixer each week to conduct the inspection with him. The two of them look at how well we are wearing our uniforms, how tidy is our hair, how clean are our fingernails, and how shiny are our shoes. We then receive a score for our six.

I do not do very well in these inspections, and sometimes our six gets the lowest scores because of me. I try to be smartly dressed, but I often can't find all the bits of my uniform and sometimes, not always, my fingernails are not very clean. I don't like washing my hands and I hate having a bath because of my eczema, but I will try to become a cleaner cub so that I don't let my six down.

Akela was the first person ever to call me 'Tony'. Until I joined the cubs, everybody called me Anthony, but on my first night, Akela asked me to tell everybody my name. I said that my name was Anthony, and he then said that they would call me Tony from now on. And Tony it is – at least at cubs. My teachers still call me Anthony, though, and my mam and dad.

When I started the cubs, I was a 'tenderpad'. After a few weeks, I was 'invested' and I got a badge that my mam sewed on to my jumper. Then, after I had completed some tasks, I got my first silver star. That went on to my cap to the left of the badge.   That meant that one of my eyes was 'open', and I was no longer a tenderpad.

The second star followed soon afterwards, so both of my eyes were 'open' and I was a proper cub. I recently became a Seconder and I think that if I work well, and get some more badges, I might become a Sixer one day.

And now the Jamboree! Akela explains that this is a name given to a large gathering of cubs and scouts. We will meet cubs and scouts from all over the North East at The Links, in Whitley Bay, near St Mary's lighthouse. There will be games to play, some of the troops will do marching, and we will all meet Lord Rowallan, the Chief Scout.

Akela says that all the Tynemouth scout troops will be present, as well as hundreds of boys from towns and cities like Newcastle and Durham.

And the best thing is that we are all going to sleep in a tent for one night. Akela calls it 'a night under canvas'. I was thinking that it might go towards my Leaping Wolf badge, so I ask him if we will be cooking our meals on a camp fire, and he says yes, of course we will. If I offer to help with the cooking, I could get another part of my badge, the 'cooking a meal' part, and if I get to light the fire, that could be all my Outdoorsman badge tests completed.

Akela says no. Although we will be doing all the things that he has mentioned, sleeping out, lighting a fire, cooking meat and so on, we will be doing them together as a troop. The Leaping Wolf badges, especially the Outdoorsman badge, must be done in the wild, so they will not count towards a badge. He then smiles and says that I could do my Outdoorsman badge in our back garden – 'that is wild enough', and some of the other boys snigger. They know that the front and back gardens at my house are a mess because my dad won't do anything to them, and my mam can't because she is going to have a baby very soon.

I am slightly disappointed that our night under canvas won't count towards my leaping wolf badge, but still I am looking forward to the Jamboree. I have never spent a night under canvas, I have never even spent a night away from my family – at least, away from my mam – except when she went into hospital to have Glenda, so I think that the adventure will make up for any disappointment I might feel about not getting my Leaping Wolf badge just yet.

I like the cubs so much that I have already decided that when I am eleven, I will become a Boy Scout. There is so much to learn, and I can't understand how my friends prefer to play out every evening, playing the same daft games, doing the same boring things night after night. The Cubs do different things each week, and I look forward to our pack meetings.

Because I also sing in the choir at St George's Cullercoats, I already know two or three boys who are scouts. They are in the Fifth Whitley Bay Troop, and they meet in their own scout hut on Links Road. That is not far from where I live and as I cross Links Road every time I go to choir practice, I know exactly where the scout hut is. That is the troop that I will join when I have to leave the cubs at the age of eleven.

***

I went the Jamboree on Saturday, and we stayed in our tent overnight. Nine others from my cub pack went. Akela has just walked back home with me and his son, Reg. He helped me bring my kit bag back home, as I could not carry it, what with my hand being bandaged and the kit bag being so heavy.

He has just told my mam that it was not a good idea for him to take us to the Jamboree. We were too young to appreciate it, he says. Too many silly boys, and too much excitement. I was one of the silly boys, I suppose, but he didn't say so. At home, I call him Mr Carr, but at cubs he is 'Akela'. When he talks about cub things at my house, I don't know which name to use.

Mam has been looking at my hand and she asks Mr Carr what happened to me.

He says it is a long story. It's not a long story. I say that I was left alone to make a fire, and Mr Carr (Akela) interrupts me and says he had better explain, and that there is something else that he wants to discuss with my mam.

Mam looks at Mr Carr, and then she asks me to go out and play for a while, and I see David Brown out of the window. I say that I can go and play with him. Mam says that is fine, and that she wants me back here for tea. Akela asks Reg if he would like to and play also, but Reg says no, he is tired, and he is going home to sleep.

I go out to play with David. David is not in the cubs. His mam won't let him join. He has joined the Boys' Brigade because his dad was in it, and now he is learning to play the bugle. I like David, and I often play with him. When we used to play Davey Crockett, we pricked our fingers with a needle and became 'blood brothers', just like the Indians do. I am quite sad that he didn't join the cubs, but he is not sad about it at all. He says that the Boys' Brigade is better than the cubs, because 'the cubs is for babies'.

I try to explain to David the kind of things that we do at cubs, and I tell him about the Jamboree, but David just laughs, 'The Boys' Brigade is better than anything the cubs do. My dad said so – so there!'

He picks up his football and we cross the road to the strip of grass where we play, while Reg goes into his house to see his mam. David asks me about the bandage on my hand, and I tell him that I burned it at the Jamboree. He asks if I am all right to play, and I say of course I am.

David loves football – even more than I do. He's very good and he plays in the school team even though he is only eight. He is the youngest player ever to play in the school team, and our head teacher, Mrs Statham, says that she has 'made an exception' because David is so good.

We soon forget our argument about the cubs and the Boys Brigade because Stephen Robson joins us, and we have a kickabout. Although I love it, I am not very good at football, so while we play, kicking the ball, tackling each other, scoring goals, my mind is thinking about what Mr Carr is saying to my mam, and how he thought that we were 'too young to appreciate' the Jamboree. He will be explaining how I burned my hand, and I know that she won't be very pleased with me.

I see that Mrs Carr has just come out of her house, and she is walking down to where I live. She is standing at the gate with her arms folded. Akela must have seen her as he has just come out of my house quite quickly. He and Mrs Carr are now walking back up the road. Mrs Carr does not seem to be very happy to see Akela, and she did not wait for him before she turned to go back to her house. Akela is following her and asking her what is the matter.

It has been a busy weekend, and I am also very tired. I will go to bed early. On Friday night, I had to pack my things for the Jamboree. My dad had given me his old army kit bag to use, and my mam had found a sleeping bag somewhere in the wash house, which I had never seen before. I also had a red plastic mug, a plastic plate and my own knife, fork and spoon. Oh, and my swimming trunks, a proper pair – much better than the woollen ones I used to have – plus a towel and some soap.

On the Saturday morning, when I tried to pick the kit bag up, I couldn't lift it. My dad said that he would help me carry it to the church; my mam gave me a kiss and said that I should be good and that I should take care. Then my dad walked with me up to St Hilda's where all the cubs were to meet at ten o'clock.

Akela had said that we were going on a 'trek', and I wasn't quite sure what that meant. It turns out that a trek means that we were going on the back of a lorry, and we had to load up the lorry with our 'kit'. There were ten of us going, and we were to sit on the back of the lorry on top of the kit.

We loaded two tents on to the lorry - Akela had borrowed the tents from a scout troop. He had also borrowed some cooking pots – he calls them billies, some rope and some long wooden poles. He said that these things would all come in handy at the Jamboree.

It was difficult to find a comfortable place to sit on the lorry as there were no sides on it. That meant that we could not lean our backs against anything and had to sit or lie face down on the kit that we had loaded. I found quite a good place near the tents, but I saw that one or two of the other boys were a bit frightened as the lorry started up and moved away from St Hilda's and down Wallington Avenue.

Nobody fell off the lorry on our way to Whitley Bay, and when we arrived, I understood what Akela had told us about how many people would be there. There were hundreds of cubs and scouts – all in uniform, all with different neckerchiefs, different hats and caps, and all trying to put up their tents in the space that been given to their troop.

Our lorry stopped where all the other lorries and vans had stopped, and we had to carry all our kit, including the tents, to 'Pitch 146', which was where we were to 'pitch' our tents.

Pitch 146 was miles away – I don't know how far exactly, but it was a long way. My kit bag was so heavy that I couldn't carry it and I had to drag it along behind me. And I also had to carry one of the billy cans as well.

When we got to our camp site, Akela told us that the first thing that we were going to do was to pitch our tents. There were two tents and one was going to be for us, and the second, smaller tent was going to be for Akela. Reg Carr, his son, asked his dad if he could stay in the smaller tent as well, but his dad said no, he was a Sixer, and he had responsibilities.

I had never pitched a tent before; none of the other boys had, and I am not entirely sure that Akela knew too much about pitching tents either. He did become quite angry, and he used some swear words as well as we tried to get the tents looking the same as all the other tents around us.

Our big tent was called a 'Fourteen by Fourteen', and Akela said that this was the kind of tent that soldiers use, so it would be fine for us. It was very big and heavy, made from thick canvas – and it was very hard to get it to stand up properly, but when we had got it up, we could see that all ten of the cubs would easily be able to sleep in it. Akela's tent was much smaller, and one of the tent poles was missing. He had to use a long piece of wood as a tent pole instead, and this made him quite annoyed.

When our tents were up, we stood back and looked at them. Even I could see that they looked different from those next to us on both sides. Both of our tents drooped in the middle, the pegs holding the tents were not in straight lines, and they had different types of guy ropes; one of the guy ropes was a piece of string, but Akela said that it would have to do like that because the 'gathering' was going to begin.

The gathering was around a giant circle further down on The Links. A huge space had been made with a raised stand where a band was now playing. We put all our kit into our tent. I was given a groundsheet, and I put my sleeping bag down on it.

I made my kit bag into a kind of pillow, and then I checked my uniform. I pulled up my socks, straightened my garter tabs, made sure that my neckerchief was straight and that my hair was tidy – it was a good job I had brought a comb with me, as none of the other boys had one.

Akela then made the ten of us divide into two Sixes – although there were only five of us in each Six. I was a Seconder, and Reg Carr was the Sixer of my group. We then inspected our uniforms, and when Akela thought that we were ready, he lined us up – Sixer at the front – Seconder at the back, and we marched down to the gathering.

Our marching was not very good. Akela tried to get us to march in time, but none of us had ever marched before. We saw other groups of boys, all much more smartly dressed than we were, marching perfectly in step. They must have been practising for weeks to be that good, so Akela said to us to stop marching. He then said that we should walk quietly to the gathering, and not worry too much about being in step. This was a much better idea. We did not look quite so silly, and I was much less embarrassed.

There was a special place reserved for our pack - a sign that said, 'Pitch146'. It was in a good position. We could all sit on the ground just next to the rope that had been put around the circle of the gathering, and we could see everything.

The Scouts' brass band had been playing since we arrived at the campsite to put up our tents. They suddenly stopped, gathered all their things together and left the stage. Another band - a marching band - started to play, and into the circle they came. They also were scouts, dressed in different types of scout uniforms.

Reg Carr knew all the uniforms and he was able to say that those in light blue shirts were Air Scouts and those in dark blue tops were Sea Scouts. The rest of the band had uniforms that were like those of the scouts that I had seen at St George's, but all their neckerchiefs were different, and some wore the old-fashioned flat hats while others wore green berets which were slanted to one side.

The band that was marching around the arena had been put together from all the scouts in the region who could play musical instruments, and they were very exciting to listen to.

They marched around once more, and then they turned and marched out of the ring. As they left, a man stepped on to the raised platform that had been used as a bandstand. He had a microphone, and he called all of us to attention. We all stood up to attention, and as the flag was brought in to the circle, everybody saluted it. We were cubs, and our way of beginning was when Akela called 'Pack Pack Pack!', so we were a little slower in saluting.

We watched the older boys, the scouts, and while the flag was moving, they maintained their salutes. The scouts were saluting with three fingers, and all of us knew that we had to salute with two. I looked around, and we had all got that right. The flag was on a pole, carried by a senior scout, and he placed it at the very top of the raised platform, walked back down to the grass, turned and saluted the flag. When he completed his salute, and put down his hand, all the other scouts dropped their arms too – and so did we.

There was a silence for a few moments, and then the man with the microphone began to speak. He welcomed everybody to the Jamboree, asked us to sit, and then said that he was 'proud and privileged' to introduce us to the Chief Scout himself, Lord Rowallan.

Lord Rowallan came on to the stage. He was wearing a kilt, and he had a walking stick because he was limping. He wore one of those flat-brimmed scout hats that some of the scouts in the marching band were wearing, and he said that we were a wonderful sight. He had been to many jamborees, he said, and he was always impressed by the sight of so many fine young men in uniform.

We were here to celebrate the success of the scouting movement, and he said that he had heard many tales of how helpful we were to members of the community.

He wished us well with our future and promised us that the skills that we would learn as scouts (he did not mention cubs) would be valuable skills for the rest of our lives.

He then asked us to say the Scout Promise. Everybody began, but we cubs all got it wrong. The last two lines of our Promise are:

'To keep the law of the wolf cub pack

And to do a good deed to somebody every day.'

The last lines of the Scout Promise are different from ours, and we did not know them. I realise that when I become a scout, I will need to know the new words, but it did not seem to matter this time as the Promise was soon over.

Lord Rowallan saluted us, and then he left the stage. He shook hands with a few people, scouts, scoutmasters – and some important looking people wearing ordinary suits. He then got into the back seat of a car – a big black Austin16 with a driver – and that was it, he was gone. I thought that Akela had said that we all were going to meet him. I had a question to ask him about the Leaping Wolf badge, but I never had the opportunity to ask it.

But the afternoon had not finished. There were lots of displays for us to watch: there was a fire-lighting competition, which the Air Scouts won – their team was the fastest to boil a billy of water - some senior scouts showed their axemanship skills, chopping tree trunks, splitting logs and showing how to use different axes properly.   There was a Trek Cart race: this was great to see – the teams had to run to a line with their trek cart, dismantle it completely and carry the pieces across an imaginary river, and then reassemble the cart.

The Axemanship display was one that I also liked. We were shown how to care for our axe. We were shown the different kinds of axe: small axes – hatchets - and larger axes, felling axes. How you stand, how you hold the axe, how you swing a felling axe – all of us were shown how to do these tasks correctly. There are badges for axemanship in the scouts, both first and second-class tests. You are not allowed to use a hatchet until you have passed your second class axemanship, and you must not use a felling axe until you have your first-class badge.

I want to be able to chop firewood for my grandma and grandad. When I am a scout, I can get my axemanship badges and then I will be able to do the chopping instead of Grandad doing it because I know he hates that job.

I also found out that when I join the scouts, and pass my axemanship and woodcraft badges, I will be able to wear a sheath knife as part of my uniform. I will ask my Uncle Tom if I can have one for my birthday present. I will ask him because he often buys presents for me.

When I broke my arm, he bought me a five-battery torch. The beam was so strong it went for miles. I wish I had brought it here this weekend, but the batteries have run out, and my mam said that new ones were too expensive.

As we walk down to the arena, we pass all the stalls that are selling things that might interest scouts. One stall really interested me. It sells torches of all different sizes, but also it sells scout knives. I am only a cub and know that they would not sell a knife to me, but if I was a scout I know that I could buy a sheath knife today. The knife that I want has a leather handle and a leather sheath. I will be able to wear it on my scout belt, and I will sharpen it and polish it: I am sure that it will come in very useful.

There are other knives that scouts can buy too. The Swiss Army Knife has lots of blades. It can be used as a screwdriver and as a pair of scissors, but it does not look as stylish as the sheath knife, and it is very expensive. The stall also sells big black clasp knives. These have a marlin spike as well as a blade, so with all those knives on display there is quite a big choice, but I know the one I want to have – a leather handled sheath knife with a four-and-a-half-inch blade – nothing else.

When I get my new knife, I will carry it when I go to choir practice. I hate going down that lane to St George's church when it is dark, and usually I take my gun with me.

It's not a real gun, but it looks real. It is a blue metal Beretta semi-automatic pistol. It is just a toy, but I carry it in my pocket to make me feel safe. A sheath knife will make me feel even more safe on that scary journey. I do hope that I never have to use it.

One thing I have noticed recently is that I am not very brave. I make a lot of plans for what I will do if I am attacked – that is why I have my Beretta – but when I am bullied at school, or when I think that someone might be following me, even if that is just my imagination, I start to tremble so much that I don't think that I would be able to do anything if anyone attacked me.

I liked the arena part of the Jamboree in the afternoon, but I didn't like the evening so much. We had not made any plans. When we returned to Site 146, I noticed that the well organised groups of scouts around us had already started to build their camp fires. We needed to make a fire too - this was important – if we were going to eat today, and Akela told me that that was my job to make the fire.

Freddie Sharp's dad had given us a box of kippers, we had some tins of corned beef and about six loaves of sliced white bread. There was a box of apples too, and Jimmy Ferguson, the milkman, had given us a kit of milk. (I was surprised at this, because Jimmy Ferguson insists that the Boy's Brigade is better than the scouts, but he is friends with Akela – Mr Carr.) We also had some packets of Cadbury's Smash. This is something new and I have never had it before: it is supposed to be mashed potato, but it is a powder that you add water to. Scouts think it is a great idea and it will catch on because it is so much lighter to carry on a hike than real potatoes, and it doesn't take up nearly as much space.

Our menu tonight is corned beef and mashed potato, with bread and Stork margarine – and an apple. The kippers will be for breakfast.

I was only supposed to use two matches to light the fire, and they both went out. Akela said that because of that, we wouldn't be having any tea as 'Tony failed to light the fire.'

It wasn't my fault. Akela then told me to find some silver birch bark and use that instead of paper. There is no bark on The Links – there aren't even any trees! What was I supposed to do?

He asked me to try to light the fire again, while he took the rest of the boys off for a walk around the stalls to see what was on sale. I would have like to have gone with everybody else, but Akela said that I was being given another chance to get a fire going.

My grandma uses rolled up newspaper and little sticks of wood, and her fires light every time. So, while Akela was away with the others, I found a newspaper, bits of newspaper anyway, and some leaflets that had blown over from one of the stalls. I rolled each sheet into a little tube which I tied into a knot – just like my grandma does. I then put some twigs on the newspaper tubes and lit the newspaper. The fire caught light straight away. I added some of the wood that we had brought with us, and then I decided to make tea for everyone.

I went down to the tap, which was only a few yards away, and I filled a big billy can with water. It was very heavy, but I managed to get it back without spilling anything. I then put the billy on the fire and started to pile wood around it to make the water boil faster.

I opened four tins of corned beef, and I buttered twenty-two slices of bread with Stork margarine, so that everyone could help themselves to their tea. I then decided to cook the hot part of our meal – the Cadbury's Smash, so that when everyone came back to Site 146, their tea would be ready for them.

There were instructions on the packet of Smash, but they were for saucepans, not for billy cans. The billy can was starting to bubble, so I added the contents of all six packets of Smash and stirred them with a clean stick that I had kept back specially.

It did not magically become mashed potato. There was too much water in the billy can and not enough Smash. What I had made was a white soup.

Akela arrived back with the boys, saw that the fire was working and said that I had done a good job. He saw that I had opened the cans of corned beef, and that I had buttered the bread quite well too. Then he looked at the billy can. He asked me what it was, and I said it was the Cadbury's Smash. He then looked at the boiling white soup and looked at me. He wanted to know what had happened; Cadbury's Smash wasn't meant to be like this. He had had it at home and it was just like mashed potato.

Then it happened. I saw in Akela's eyes that I had made a mistake with the Smash, and I leaned over to the billy can and grasped its handle. I screamed in pain as my hand was burned, the billy can spilled over into the fire and the white soup of Cadbury's Smash spilled into the fire putting it out and flowing on into the grass.

My hand was very sore, and I began to cry. Akela came to me, looked at my hand and said what a stupid thing it was to pick up anything from a camp fire. All the cubs around me were very quiet.

Akela said that we would go to the First Aid tent, and we walked there straight away. A kind senior scout looked at my hand, put some cream on it – the palm of my hand was scorched. He said it was not too serious, but if it still hurt on Monday I should get my mam to take me to the doctor. He then strapped my hand up with a bandage, and he told Akela that we might as well make the most of this incident and show the cubs the value of the neckerchief by using a real example. My neckerchief became a sling for my bandaged hand.

We then went back to Pitch 146. Nobody was there. The Scouter from Site 147 had seen Akela leave with me and had invited our troop to join his around the camp fire. They had taken their food, and he had fried up the corn beef and given each boy a roast potato that had been cooked in the ashes of their fire. He had even kept some corn beef and potato back for me and Akela. I enjoyed that meal – much better than Cadbury's Smash – even though I found it difficult to eat with only one hand.

We then sat around the camp fire and the scouter began to sing some songs. His scouts knew the words to all the songs, and as they were easy to learn, soon we did too.

I found out that many of the songs that they were singing that evening were from 'Gang Shows'. The scouter told us all that boys from all over came together to perform in local theatres. They sang songs, played different parts in short plays, and learned about acting and singing at the same time.

The disaster that I had created turned into a successful meal and camp fire singsong. As I sang along with the scouts, this became one of the best evenings I ever had as a cub. I knew that I would love being in a Gang Show, and I asked Akela if he could find out about how I would join one. He said that would be a good idea, as I had obviously enjoyed the singing so much. I had, and although my hand hurt, I seemed to forget about it while I was singing.

When it became dark, and we had repeated some of the songs too often, the fire began to die. That was the signal to bring our singsong to an end, and we all went into our tent to find our sleeping bags and settle down to sleep after a busy day.

Nobody slept that night. I couldn't get off to sleep because I was singing all the songs again and imagining myself on a stage in a theatre. When I did try to drop off to sleep, the nine other cubs in our tent were still wide awake, and even though Akela came in to see us, telling us to go to sleep – and he did this many times – it was impossible.

Just as I was going off, somebody would fart, or pretend to fart, or throw a shoe or a boot at a sleeping boy and everybody would wake up – again. Also, the whole tent was damp. My sleeping bag was freezing, and I am sure that the groundsheet wasn't waterproof because there was a damp patch around my feet when I got out of bed.

Breakfast the next morning was slightly more successful than the meal I had tried to cook the night before. Akela allowed me to light a new fire – he sent the other cubs off to find the wood. My bandaged hand was the main reason I stayed, but I used some newspaper to light the fire, and Akela said that I had done a really good job with that fire, and he asked me how we were going to cook the kippers.

Again, my grandma came to my rescue. She cooks kippers by putting them in boiling water for a few minutes just to warm them up. Akela said that was a great suggestion, and let's do it.

We used the same billy that I had tried to pick up from the fire yesterday and filled it half full with water.

Freddie Sharp's dad had given us a box of twelve pairs of kippers. We had three full loaves of bread left, and quite a lot of stale slices of bread were left over from last night's disastrous 'Smash' meal.

I suggested that each of us had two kippers, we had a slice of fresh bread each, and we could toast the stale bread on the fire if we wanted anything else to eat. We would boil another billy to make tea, as we still had some milk left, and if people did not want to have tea, they could drink water.

Akela said that was a great idea, and he also said that lighting the fire and cooking the kippers could count towards my Outdoorsman badge after all.

The boys came back with wood; some of them did not want the kippers, but they were happy with toast and bread. We boiled the second billy and made some tea, so everyone could have something hot for breakfast, even if it was just a cup of tea.

When we had finished our breakfast, we collected all our rubbish, put out our fire and began to take down our tents. I packed my kit bag too. My sleeping bag was soaking wet, so that when I tried to lift the kit bag, it was heavier than when I had brought it.

We had to make two journeys to the lorry, as the tents were not very well packed – and they were damp – so it took five or six people just to carry the big tent back to the lorry and heave it on board.

Eventually we all climbed on to the back of the lorry, found a place to sit or lie among our tents and the other kit, and made our way back to St Hilda's. We were all very quiet on the way back – and half asleep but worrying about falling off the lorry kept our eyes open.

***

I can't play football any longer with Stephen Robson and David – my eyes won't stay open, so I go home, and my mam says that Akela has told her something that he thought was important.

I ask her if it was about my hand; that was just an accident, and I went straight to the medical tent.

She says no – it was not about my hand. Mr Carr thinks that I have got some 'talent' – that's what he told my mam. He said that he listened very carefully to me while I was singing last night, and he saw how much I enjoyed it. He also says that I have a very good voice. He thinks that I must join the Gang Show, and mam tells me that she is very proud of me – and what do I think about joining the Gang Show next year?

I am in bed now. I have had a wash – I don't like washing because it hurts me – but I really needed one today. My mam has looked at my hand and changed the bandage – she was a nurse and knows what to do – and just before I fall asleep, I sing all the songs that we sang last night. And do you know what? I remember the words and the tunes to every one of them.

Seven

Fireworks Night

'Police arrested two kids yesterday, one was drinking battery acid, the other was eating fireworks. They charged one and let the other off.' Tommy Cooper

I always look forward to Fireworks night, although around our way it starts a lot earlier than November the fifth. We are out most evenings in October collecting stuff for our bonfire. We build the bonfire on the field at the top of the road, but it's not so easy this year.

Firstly, it's not a field any more. When we first started, when we moved in here five or six years ago, it was just a plot of waste land. It was easy to build a fire here, and it was safe. Now, with the shops on Buttermere Road completed, and with the council trying to turn that waste ground into a park with trees and paths, many people are unhappy with the bonfire being put there.

And there is another reason: a gang of boys from further up the estate keeps on attacking and destroying our bonfire. They steal our wood and all the other things we have collected to burn and take them to their own bonfire at the other end of the field near Kirklinton Road. And after school until sometimes nine o'clock, they have a guard to protect their fire. The boys up there are all much older than us, and they are very tough. I don't think it would be a good idea to make enemies of Cliff Skerr and Henry Dunn and their gang.

And that is not all – yet another threat – even if all our wood is not stolen by those boys. The dads in Wallington Avenue have dismantled the bonfire that Spanner and Corky Branton built on the grass outside their house. I hope that the dads don't do the same thing to our fire because this year, my mam has bought me a packet of fireworks.

They came in a small box with pictures on it of what is inside. It's not a very exciting selection, but I also have a brown paper bag of bangers that I bought myself. She doesn't know that – she tells me that bangers are 'just too dangerous', but I have about twelve of them. Four are called 'cannons'– they cost twice as much as the bangers, but they are worth it. They make a huge explosion.

Somebody up the road had one through their letter box the other night. She reported it to the police. This morning a policeman came to our school. He warned us and said that he would be on the lookout for any 'loutish behaviour'. I won't put a firework in anybody's letterbox, but I want to set my cannons off. I'm going to join the rest of the kids at the bonfire as soon as I have had my tea.

And then my mam says, 'And don't forget, it's confirmation class tonight.'

What? Tonight? Confirmation class is tonight, I know that – every Tuesday for eight boring weeks. But not tonight, please, not on fireworks night! They must have cancelled it, mustn't they? I try to get my mam to see reason, but all I get is, 'You are going, and that's that.'

'But Mam. It's fireworks night! I've got my fireworks and everything. I'll go next week, I promise!'

'I know you'll go next week – and you will also go tonight. I promised Father Bunker. He wants to see you about something else too, and I said I would make sure that you were there tonight.'

'You know what this means, Mam? It means that I'll miss the bonfire. It will be out – or burning right down by the time the class ends.'

'Your confirmation classes are very important,' she says, 'too important to miss – especially tonight.'

More important than bonfire night and my packet of bangers? I don't think so. And what does Father Bunker want to talk to me about, anyway? I ask my mam.

Mam is coy, and she smiles at me: 'I'm not telling you now, but we both think that you will like it.'

Father Bunker is the vicar at St Hilda's: it's our local church, and I like him, he's a very kind man. That's where I go for my confirmation classes. This is particularly annoying tonight, because the church is on Wallington Avenue next to my school. I will have to walk right past the bonfire on my way there; I have already heard loads of fireworks going off, and through my window I have seen rockets and roman candles shooting up into the air. I know I am going to miss the best bits.

When I started these classes a few weeks ago, they were at St George's church in Cullercoats. I have been a choirboy there since I was eight – for nearly two years now. The vicar at St George's suggested that I take my confirmation classes at St Hilda's because it was so much nearer to my house. It was a good idea, as I already know the place very well, and I often have to walk to St George's by myself.

To begin with, and because it was his idea, my dad promised that he would take me there on his way to the Crescent club, and on the first few occasions he did. But now he plays the piano at different clubs and hotels all over, and he can't always accompany me. I sometimes think that he has forgotten his promise, but then he surprises me. He will appear at Sunday evensong to wait for me and take me home; at other times, he will walk down to the church with me, but I never know when he will be around to go with me, or to bring me back.

I hate the last part of the walk to St George's, particularly in the winter. From Links Road, down to The Avenue there is a narrow little lane you must go down that is always dark and scary - there's no other easy way to get there. Sometimes choir practice doesn't finish until nine o'clock at night, and I don't like coming home by myself. And now, in November, it is dark when I leave the house, so it's dark all the time.

St Hilda's church is only five minutes away from Hartington Road. It is quite new; it opened in the community centre next to my school. It's not a proper church – they do church services and everything, but it isn't a church building. They hope to build a brand-new church at the top of the estate very soon. I've joined lots of things, I already go to Sunday school and I go to Cubs there too, so with confirmation classes as well that means that I go there at least two or three nights a week.

I have enjoyed joining these groups, even if confirmation class is boring – and it is. Being able to go to these clubs and events is good for me as now I get even more bored playing kick the can with the same kids every night, and some of the games we play with the girls like 'catchee kissee', make me embarrassed.

Everybody knows I have eczema, so the girls definitely don't like being 'catchee'd' by me, and if I try to 'kissee' them, they scream or pretend to be sick, so I usually just stand around doing nothing.

Some kids also play more daring games like 'knock on door'; some have started smoking, and one or two of the paper boys have been stealing packets of cigarettes from the newsagents where they work and selling them as single cigarettes. Some of the older boys and girls like to go off to do kissing and cuddling – and that doesn't interest me either. When they do that, I just mooch around until I decide to go back home.

Sometimes though, we do things that make me laugh: I did enjoy it last week when we dressed up Corky Branton as a Guy, put him in an old pram, and Spanner and me took him to all the houses in his street asking for a 'penny for the Guy'.

Lots of people didn't guess that it was Corky; some did of course. We collected two and fourpence altogether, mostly in pennies, and I expected that we would split it three ways, but Spanner and Corky kept the two bob and I got the rest - fourpence.

My confirmation class starts at seven o'clock, and I am a little late. There are three other people in the class, two girls and a very old lady. I am late because I stopped at the bonfire for a few minutes. One of the boys, Bruce Fraser, saw my box of fireworks and asked me if I was going to set them off. I told him, no, I had to go to the church first, but when I finish my confirmation class, I will set them off.

He laughed when he heard what I was doing - and where I was going. He says that nobody will ever catch him in a church, but he also says that he has made a fireworks gun, and that he is going to use it tonight. I ask him what it was, and he says he will show me later – when I finish my class.

I have to wait until the end of the class, just before half past eight, before Father Bunker tells me the thing that he and Mam have been keeping secret. He wants me to be a shepherd in the nativity play at St George's just before Christmas – that's the surprise that Mam was talking about. He says that because I have such a good speaking voice, I will be 'ideal' for the part. He has typed the lines I am to say:

'The voice of him that crieth in the wilderness. Prepare ye the way of the Lord.   Make straight in the desert a pathway for our God.'

I am to be dressed as a shepherd; my mam has already agreed to make me a shepherd's costume, and Father Bunker says that he has told my mam that he will take me to rehearsals himself, as he is producing the play.

Mam said that I would be pleased by this – and I am. I love the idea of being in a play; I am nervous, but excited at the same time. We start rehearsals next week, and I say that yes, I will say the lines – and wear the shepherd's costume, but can I go now, please? My mates are waiting for me so that we can light my fireworks, and I show him my box of fireworks - but not the bangers.

He says yes, of course I can go. The class is over. I am to be careful with those fireworks, and I should make sure that an adult is around when I set them off. Both he and I know that is not going to happen, but I suppose he had to say something like that.

Bruce Fraser and his brother are waiting outside the hall when I leave. I am quite surprised by this. I did tell Father Bunker that my mates were waiting for me, but I didn't expect anybody to be there. And Bruce is not a mate: I know him, but we don't play together, and he doesn't go to the same school as me. His family live in a flat above one of the shops in Buttermere Road, and his dad has a fish and chip shop there.

They have only been on the Marden for a few months, and he still goes to another school in Whitley Bay. He's the boy I talked to on my way here, and who said that he had made a fireworks gun.

'Have you still got those fireworks?'

'Yes,' I'm carrying them in the paper bag, he's seen them. There's nothing else to say.

'Let's see what you've got, then.' And he snatches the bag from me. He opens it. There is the little box in there – the fireworks that Mam bought me. In the box are sparklers, Catherine wheels, a couple of small roman candles and one titchy rocket.   He's not interested in those, but he pokes his hand into the bag and brings out some of my bangers.

'These'll do.' He turns to Jeff, his brother as he rummages in the bag for the rest of the bangers. 'Come on, we'll try these.' He looks at me. 'You can come if you want to.'

'They're my bangers. Give them back!'

Jeff laughs. His brother takes the bag, throws back the box of fireworks that my mam bought for me and says, 'You can play with these if you want. We don't want them.'

'What are you going to do with my bangers'? I am panicking now. I paid for those myself with my own money. I don't want to lose them: I have been thinking about tonight for weeks.

'I said you could come with us if you want to – they are your bangers, after all.'

I think about this. I assume that they are going to use my bangers with their fireworks gun. They are not carrying the gun with them, but they must have been waiting outside to get my bangers, as there is no other reason why they would wait for me. My choice is simple: I either go with them and see what they plan to do, or I lose my bangers, and never see or hear them going off. It's not a difficult choice to make.

'Where are you going now?' I say.

'Just on the field. Over there.'

You can see the field from here – the field where the bonfires are. There are – I should say there were – two of them, and you can still see a glow, but the main fires have burned down now. I can also see the shadows of a few people around, but nobody has any fireworks left now. I am too late.

Except for my own fireworks: it seems that they are the only ones left on the whole estate. And Bruce and Jeff have just taken the best ones from me. I decide – 'Yes, I'll come with you. I want to see what you are doing.'

He smiles, 'Good. I didn't want to steal them from you.'

I am surprised at this. I thought that was exactly what he wanted to do. He then adds, 'And we want somebody to hold the target.' And they both laugh as they set off towards the field and the dying bonfires.

I follow the two boys as they make their way to the field. They walk ahead of me: they know that I am there, but they keep separate from me – laughing and sniggering at jokes they make, bashing each other on the arm or aiming a kick at each other's bum. Bruce has all my bangers, and he has put them in his trouser pockets so that he can fight with his brother on the way.

When we get to the field, Bruce and Jeff don't go to one of the bonfires, they go to what looks like an unlit bonfire. But it is not, it is a pile of bricks and stones that the council has cleared from the field. They hope to make it a park with grass and flowers one day, and they have started by trying to make it more level and getting all the stones and rocks gathered together.

Bruce bends down and picks up his 'gun'. He shows it to me. It is just like a rifle; the barrel is longer. It is a copper pipe, maybe five feet long, and it has a wooden grip that has been tied to the barrel by wire. When Bruce puts it on his shoulder, you can see how it works. The barrel reaches way behind Bruce's shoulder, and is open at both ends, the front and the rear.

'How do you fire it?' My first question; indeed, the first thing that I have said since we set off from St Hilda's.

'These are the bullets,' says Bruce, taking a handful of glass marbles from his pocket. In his hand, there are also some ball bearings – we call them 'steelies'.

'It's the steelies that work best, they fly for miles,' he continues, 'I bet I could fire one of these the whole length of the field.'

Jeff picks up a large square piece of wood. It's an old door panel, but it has a hole in it the size of my head. 'The gun did that. Just think what it would do to a person – what it would do to you!' They both laugh.

'That's why we want you to be the target; we'll put a hole straight through you – see what your mam thinks of that!' And he laughs gain and Bruce gets him in a neck hold and they start to fight again.

Bruce, while holding his bother down says, 'He's just kidding. That would kill you – the steelie would go straight through you, it would kill anyone. It's amazing, far better than we thought it would be.'

I am relieved that they are not going to use me as the target, but I want to see the gun in action. 'So, what are you going to fire it at?

'This.' says Jeff, and he moves a couple of yards towards the pile of stones and drags a metal box over to Bruce and me. I've seen one of these before; my Uncle Tom has one when he goes away to sea. My uncle's box is shiny and brightly painted, but even in the dark we can see that this box is old and rusty.

Together we pull and push at it until the box is standing on one end. Then Bruce says that will do and he gets the gun ready. He stands up straight and puts the barrel of the gun over his shoulder, pointing it at the box. He is about ten yards away from it. Jeff moves behind Bruce, takes one of my bangers and puts it in the pipe behind Bruce. He then moves in front of Bruce and places one of the steelies in the front of the pipe.

He then tells Bruce to wait, and he moves behind him again, and holds the fuse of the banger – still in the pipe – and says 'Right.' to Bruce. Bruce then lifts the front of the pipe, allowing the steelie to roll down the pipe until it reaches the banger.   Bruce then adjusts the pipe until it is aimed at the metal box.

Jeff says, 'OK. Here we go.' and he takes a box of matches out of his pocket, sets light to the banger and stands to one side.

There is a huge bang as the firework explodes, but what happens to the steelie is amazing. It hits the metal box, but doesn't just go straight through it, it shatters it. The box is so rusty that its hinges break off and we are left with something that looks as if a tractor has run over it.

'And that was with a banger, not a cannon.' says Bruce.' Let's try a cannon now.'

Jeff is very keen, I am not so sure. That gun is dangerous; somebody could get killed. Every year where we live, someone gets hurt trying to pick up a banger or a firework that has not exploded. My mam has told me about this a dozen times, but this. She would go crazy if she knew that I had bangers – never mind that I was playing with boys who were making a gun.

I decide to leave, but I want to take my fireworks with me. 'I've got to go now,' I tell Bruce, 'Me mam will be wondering where I am.'

'You're gonna miss the best bit,' says Bruce. He has sorted out the cannons from the other bangers. I know that there are four of them. Jeff is looking for another target, and he has put a large glass jar on top of a pole and stuck the pole in the ground. The glass jar is about six feet off the ground, and that is the next target. Bruce is going to fire the gun at the glass jar.

'You better stand back, kidda,' he says to me. 'This is going to explode everywhere. Right, Jeffrey boy, we will use the cannon this time.'

'Can I have my bangers back?' I say this with no great expectation of success, and I am surprised when Jeff says, 'We'll keep the cannons – you can have the rest.'

That is a better result than I thought I would get, and I say ok, pick up my bangers and begin to walk away. I hope they don't decide to target me.

I hear the cannon go off – and I immediately tense my shoulders and wait for the steelie to hit me, but it doesn't. I am not the target. I turn around to see if the glass jar has been hit, and then I hear the crash of glass, but it's not the glass jar – it is still standing on the pole.

The noise I hear is the sound of a shopfront window being shattered. I am hearing the shards of glass as the whole of the big window falls to the ground. The steelie has travelled way past its target, the glass jar on the pole, and has gone straight through the window of Carrick's the bakers.

I look along the parade of shops on Buttermere Road. Three shops down, Bruce Fraser's dad has just come out on to the street from his chip shop. It is the only shop open at this time of night and there are customers in it. I realise immediately that if the steelie had landed there, instead of at the baker's, someone could have been seriously hurt.

There is no sign of Bruce or of Jeff, and I can't see anything of the gun.

A few people are now standing outside Carrick's, looking at the damage and trying to work out what has happened. They are looking on to the field and towards the two dead bonfires, but nobody is around.

They will blame me. I know it! I had the cannons, and I still have eight bangers in my bag – and the box of fireworks that my mam gave me.

I decide that I must get rid of the bangers in case someone comes to ask me about what has happened. I won't know what to say. I didn't fire the gun, but it was my cannon that they used.

I have almost arrived at my house when I decide what I will do. I will keep my fireworks, the ones that Mam bought for me, and I will hide the bangers. I will hide them in the wash house - nobody will think of looking there. I quietly sneak into the wash house, and working entirely in the dark, I find some pieces of wood leaning against the wall. I put the bangers there – I can come back tomorrow and find a better hiding place if I need to.

I then go into my house by the back door. My dad is out, but my mam is sitting by the fire reading her book and smoking her cigarette. She looks up.

'Hello Chicken – are you all right?'

'Yes, Mam. I've just finished confirmation class. I came straight home.'

'Did you go to the bonfire?'

'No, everything was finished by the time the class ended. There was no point'

Did you not go on the field with your fireworks?'

Then I tell a lie, 'No, there was nobody there, so I just came straight back home.'

'What about your fireworks?' Then she sees that I am holding the box. 'Have you still got them?'

'Yes, I've not set them off.'

'Do you want to do that now, pet? We can set them off in the back garden.'

'Naaa, I'm not that bothered. I think I'll go to bed.'

'Give me the box,' Mam says, and I hand it to her. 'I'll put my cardie on and we'll go out the back. You have been looking forward to this for months. I'm sorry that the confirmation class has stopped you having any fun. Did Father Bunker speak to you?'

'Yes,' I reply, 'He's asked me to be in the nativity play.'

'You will love that, Anthony, you are a very lucky boy.'

I am not feeling lucky, I am feeling sick with worry. Somebody is going to knock on the door soon, someone will find out that I was with the boys who fired the gun at the shop window.

My mam takes me outside into the back garden and waits patiently while I set off the two Catherine wheels, the two roman candles and the small rocket – which I place inside a milk bottle to steady it. We then both light a sparkler and make shapes in the air before my mam says that it is time that we go indoors.

The knock on the door comes the next night – I have spent a whole night and a day worrying about what is going to happen. It is a policeman, and he asks my mam if he could ask a few questions about me.

The two Fraser boys, Bruce and Jeff, were making a gun to fire steelies, the policeman tells my mam, and one of those steelies was fired at the window of Carrick's the bakers. Did my mam know if I was out playing last night up on the field where the incident happened?

'My Anthony?' she says. 'On the field misbehaving? Certainly not. He was at confirmation class with Father Bunker. Then he came straight home and we set off his fireworks here in the back garden.'

'Oh.' says the policeman, 'The boys we have caught say that they were with another young lad who had some bangers with him, but they don't know his name. We're asking all the families around to see if we can find out who this boy is.'

'Well you won't find him here. As I said, he was at confirmation class and then he came straight back here to me. Have you asked Father Bunker up at St Hilda's?'

'No Madam' he says, 'that won't be necessary. I'm sorry to bother you. Your son wasn't involved. Thanks for your help.' And off he went, looking for that elusive third boy.

Bruce Fraser saved me. He could have told them my name, but he chose not to.

It takes me a day or so for my nerves to settle down. I don't see Bruce and the policeman doesn't return. That great weight that was pressing down on me starts to lighten, and soon I can think of dressing in my shepherd's costume and saying the lines that Father Bunker has prepared for me.

Eight
Hugh Tweed and his Model Buses

'The imaginary friends I had as a kid dropped me because their friends thought I didn't exist'. Aaron Machado

Reg Carr, the Akela in my wolf cub pack, has noticed that I was an enthusiastic singer at a camp fire singsong that we had attended. He has a word with my mam.

'Your Anthony's got a good voice, you know. He might be interested in the Gang Show.'

We're sitting in our house at Hartington Road. Mr Carr has come down from his house a few doors up the street because he says he has an idea that my mam might be interested in.

'Our Anthony's not very musical. Stan and I both play the piano, but Anthony's not interested, are you pet?'

I shrug my shoulders – It's the piano I hate, not music. I can't get both of my hands to work together no matter how hard I try. My dad has given up trying to teach me; my mam did try to get me to learn to read music, but she too doesn't bother now.

Mr Carr continues, 'It may be that he's musical in another way. I watched him at the singsong - and I also listened to his singing. He picks up tunes very well, and he can hold a note.'

I don't know what that means, but my mam does, and she says, 'Do you think so? We've been sending him to St George's – Stan wanted him to join the choir – he seems to like it. You like the choir, don't you, Anthony?'

'It's all right,' I say, but the truth is I don't really like the choir either. I have been going now for nearly two years and I still don't have a medal. The choirmaster is Mr Haines, and his son is called David. David Haines is younger than me and he already has a medal. It's not fair and I was thinking of leaving.

I haven't told my mam and dad yet, and I am in a bit of a fix over this. I know that I want to leave the choir, but I am not sure if I should because there are at least two very good reasons why I should stay.

The first reason for me to stay is that I get paid to be a choirboy. Every three months each of us gets paid five shillings, and I have got used to having that money. I have not told my mam and dad about it, so I can spend it on sweets and goes on the machines at the Spanish City without anybody knowing. Also, if I sing at a wedding on a Saturday, I get paid an extra two and sixpence. So, if I do leave the choir – and I do want to, I will lose some money.

I have to balance that against the things that I don't like about choir, and when I think of it, there are more things that I don't like than there are things that make me want to continue.

The money is the main thing that makes me want to continue – simple. But then I think of the things that make me want to leave. Things that I don't like – the David Haines medal thing for one – that really annoys me, but the most important reason why I don't like choir is the journey to St George's from my house. It's the last part that I really hate.

I still have to walk down there, always by myself now, because taking me there is another thing my dad has given up on. It is often dark and cold, and I hate the long narrow lane that I must walk down to get to the church. I sometimes carry my toy gun, my steel blue Beretta, with me, but that doesn't really make me feel safe.

And choir practice is boring, and the church is so cold. They never have any heating on during the week, and when we sing, we can see our breath, just as if we were singing outside.

But there is a second reason that I feel that I ought to stay in the choir. That reason is a man called Hugh Tweed. He has become a kind of friend. He lives in Whitley Bay, and everybody in the choir thinks that he is strange. He is. Nobody else can talk to him except me. At least, he won't usually talk to anybody at all, but he does try to talk to me.

Hugh Tweed lives with his mother and he takes choir practice sometimes instead of Mr Haines. He is old, maybe twenty or twenty-five - I don't really know his age. However, he is a fantastic musician and he plays the piano and the organ better than anybody I have ever heard, including my mam and dad.

But he can't speak to people; he always looks frightened when he conducts the choir practice, and when somebody asks him a question, he can't look them in their eye. This always causes the other person to stop talking and move away, feeling embarrassed.

With his music, he is brilliant – even I am excited by how well he plays, but I seem to be the only person he wants to talk to. His mother, who brings him and then takes him home when choir practice has finished has noticed the way that Hugh talks to me. She says that I am the only person he ever talks to, and he looks forward to coming to St George's so that he can talk to me.

I don't understand this at all. It's not that we chat – I say hello to him and he replies - sometimes. Not much else happens, but I know that he is a very shy man, so I try to be kind to him and I do not move away when he tries to talk to me.

I feel that when he does talk, he has practised what he is going to say. The words don't sound natural – they sound as if he has been rehearsing them, like a script in a play.

This Hugh Tweed reason is quite an important one, but still, I have decided that it is not important enough. I will stop going to choir and lose the money I earn. It is not worth the effort that I have to put in – choir practice, morning and evening services on Sundays, and some Saturday afternoons too.

Going down that dark lane at night is something I am beginning to dread too. Instead, I will find out more about the Gang Show because Mr Carr is very enthusiastic, and he has said that he thinks I would be great in it. I don't think that they care one way or another down at choir – apart from Hugh Tweed, that is.

I decide to find out some more. 'Mr Carr,' I say, as he is only 'Akela' when he is wearing his uniform, 'You've said that I would like the Gang Show? I've heard of it, but I don't know much about it. What is it?'

Mr Carr smiles at Mam and then he looks at me' Anthony, I am sure that you would love it. I think that the Gang Show is one of the best things that scouting can offer a young lad like you.'

'What does it involve, Reg?

I'm glad my mam asked Mr Carr this question because although I am very interested, I have no idea what he is talking about. What would I have to do? Is it the same as choir? I want to find out.

Mr Carr seems happy to explain, 'The Gang Show is musical theatre. We put on performances, on a stage and in front of an audience. Scouts from all over the region must audition before they can join, but if they get in, they get to perform at one of the big theatres. There are sketches, dance routines and songs – sometimes there are solo songs, but most of the songs are sung by the chorus - some of the songs that we sang at the campfire last weekend were Gang Show songs.'

I remember singing those songs that night at the Jamboree. 'This Christmas the Gang Show will be at the Essoldo in Whitley Bay.' I know the Essoldo as well. It is a cinema most of the time, in Whitley Bay, but I know that there are theatre shows on there too. I have never been, but Nigel Mackay went to a pantomime there once.

'But why Anthony, Reg?' My mam is interested now.

'Anthony is a musical boy. He might have some talent, and I think that this is too good a chance to miss. If he goes to the audition, the producers will be able to tell us whether I am right. They will know if Anthony is musical or not.'

'I know that already – we all know that already. He's not musical, are you Anthony? Reg, we have tried, but he hates the piano. Stan and I have tried to teach him; he doesn't show any interest.'

'Maybe you are right, Mac, but it could be it's just the piano that he doesn't like. There are lots of other musical instruments that might interest him as he gets older.'

Mr Carr seems quite determined. 'Take our Reg - he isn't musical, and we do know that, so we don't push him. He's not interested in the Gang Show, and I must admit that we are a little disappointed – I love it so much – it would be great to have him come along to rehearsals. But, he loves sports and he's very good at football and because he's big, I think he's going to make a fine rugby player. We know that music doesn't interest him at all.

'I think your Anthony is different - he might not be able to play the piano, but I've watched him sing. You should give him the chance to audition. If it doesn't work out, I will be happy to apologise and say that you were quite right all the time.' He smiles at my mam again.

'Ok, Reg, you win.' My mam is smiling too. 'You might be right. What if I say yes?'

'If you say yes, I'll put him up for an audition for the Christmas production in Whitley Bay. The audition will be in North Shields, at Christ Church Hall, where the Scouts meet.'

'He can get a bus direct to Christ Church,' says my mam, 'but he won't be able to go to rehearsals in Whitley Bay. It's too far.'

'It's only necessary to go to Whitley Bay for the performances, and I've already thought about that,' says Mr Carr, still smiling. 'I've done my homework, you see. There is another boy on the Marden, Michael Brandreth. Michael is going to be in the Gang Show again as he was in it last year. His dad has a car and Mr Brandreth can take Anthony as well as Michael – but he's got to get through the auditions first, mind. So, Anthony will have to make his way to the first audition, but if he passes, Mr Brandreth will be happy to give him a lift whenever he takes Michael.'

If I do pass the audition, Akela tells me, rehearsals will be once a week until December, and then there might be two or more rehearsals a week until the weekend before the show. There might be extra rehearsals over that weekend, and the performances will take place over five nights –Tuesday until Saturday – all in the third week of December. Am I interested?

Am I interested? Of course, I am. Last year I was in a Nativity play at St George's church. I only had to say a few lines, but I wore a shepherd's costume and I carried a crook too. I really enjoyed doing that. Many of the other people in the play were scared of performing in public, but I loved being nervous. It made me alert and bright – I was excited because I wanted to perform, and for the first time, I enjoyed going down to St George's church, even going down the lane.

Eventually, my mam says yes, that if Mr Brandreth could take me to rehearsals along with Michael, she would be happy for me to have the chance. She also says that if I do pass the audition, I might have to give up the choir, as both rehearsing for the Gang Show and being in the choir will be too much for me.

I might be able to give up the choir without annoying mam and dad – I like that idea.

Hugh Tweed has asked me if I would like to come to his house on Saturday. I am thinking about that.

***

I go to the audition held at the Scout headquarters of the First Tynemouth troop, in the hall next to Christ Church in North Shields. Completely by chance, I also meet Ted Potts, the man who started the Gang Shows on Tyneside.

He is quite a famous person, and he must have auditioned hundreds of boys. He was there to see some other people, scouters and adults – but he sat in on the auditions for a while, and he was there when it was my turn.

I thought it was quite easy, the audition. I am asked to go into a room where three or four men, all in Scout uniform are sitting. I stand next to a piano where another man asks me what songs I know. I know the famous scout song, 'We're riding along on the crest of a wave' so I tell him, and he starts to play it immediately.

'When you are ready, Tony,' they already know my cub name – I am 'Anthony' to everybody else, but Tony in the cubs – 'just join in the chorus of the song' – and I do.

By the time we get to 'We'll do the hailing, while other ships around us sailing', I have found the notes and I sing to the accompaniment of the piano. I see Mr Potts making a note. The man who is conducting the auditions, a man with a very big moustache which is curled up at the ends, then says, 'Thank you, Tony. We'll write to you in a few days and we will let you know – but I want to say that I like your singing.'

And he does. About five or six days after the audition, I receive a letter addressed to 'Mr Tony Hunt'. It has been signed by a 'William Watson Todd' – the man with the moustache, and the letter says that my audition has been successful and that he would like me to attend rehearsals for the Gang Show.

These rehearsals will be held at the same place that I had my audition, but the performances in December will take place at the Essoldo cinema in Whitley Bay.

***

Looking at this event so many years after it happened – that invitation to join the Gang Show changes my world. This change does not happen immediately; I have a huge destructive event in my family followed by a rather tricky adolescence to negotiate. Those matters impact hugely on my education, so then I have to catch up after I have blown the first few years of secondary school - passing the eleven plus, but completely wasting the opportunity.

When - by the skin of my teeth - I reach the sixth form, I do start to develop a deep love for literature and the theatre; and I realise that I have some talent for performance. But receiving that letter inviting me to join the Gang Show, gives me the first ever indication that maybe I have some kind of potential.

The fact that I had not taken to learning to play the piano did not mean that I was a complete failure – 'the boy with the tin ear' – as my dad so often said.

***

I mentioned that Hugh Tweed has invited me to his house on Saturday afternoon. His mam asked him to ask me at choir practice, when we were going home. I said I would ask my mam if I can go, and when I get home, I ask her, and she says yes, she could do with the rest.

On Saturday, I need to take the number twelve bus to Whitley Bay, change at the bus station and take the number five which goes to St Mary's Lighthouse. The street that Hugh lives in is next to a bus stop, and I get off and walk up to his house.

When he opens the door, he says hello – but does not look at me. 'Come in,' he says. And then, 'My mother says that she will give you a ride in the car back to the bus station.' Not his dad, his mam. I don't think that there is a Mr Tweed – and he tells me what his mother is going to do almost as if he had learned some lines for a play.

Hugh then asks me if I would like to see his buses.

'What buses?' I say, as I do not understand what he means.

'I thought you had come to see the buses,' says Hugh. 'Come and have a look.'

Hugh's house is very big – it is a private house, not a council house like ours, and when he takes me into another room, I see that the whole of the room is his to play in.

He is an adult now, he must be well over twenty years old, I think, but the downstairs room he has taken me to is filled with toys that he must have collected as he grew up. All sorts of toys: a green Raleigh bicycle, a spinning top, piles of board games like Monopoly – a game called 'Rich Uncle' that I have played at school, some very old sports equipment, boots of various kinds, racquets and bats.

But it is not the toys that catch my eye, and not the piles of books either. I try to work out what I am looking at – and as I slowly make sense of it, I am astounded by what I see. The whole of the room is taken up by a huge table. It was probably three or four tables put together, and on them is what looks like a giant map – a map of the roads of Tynemouth, North Shields and Whitley Bay.

But it is not a map, as it has buildings and features which I recognise. I look more carefully at it, and it's a model of the whole area. I see the main landmarks immediately. The castle and the Collingwood Monument, Northumberland Square, the Spanish City, St George's church. I see the outdoor swimming pool at Tynemouth – everything is so carefully made and painted to look real. Hugh has modelled King Edward's Bay in such a way that it appears to have stairs, ramps and all – even little people going for a swim or the beach – and then I see Hartington Road.

'That's where I live. Hartington Road.'

'Yes,' says Hugh, 'And you are on a main bus route.'

'A bus route? What do you mean?' Then, before he answers, I notice maybe ten or more little red double decker buses all over the model, and I see one or two single deckers too. Each bus is on one of the roads that Hugh has laid out in his model. One of them is halfway up Hartington Road.

'What you are looking at,' says Hugh – again as if he is reading from a book, as what he is saying has no 'life' to it, and he seems to be reading words that he doesn't understand. But he's not reading – this is how he speaks. 'What you are looking at is the route system of the

Tynemouth and District Transport Company Limited, and the buses you can see are exactly the same as the buses that the company uses.

They are exact replicas - and where you see them on my model is where they are at each hour of the day.'

He continues, 'If you look carefully, you will see that each bus is registered, and that each registration number is accurate.'

He points to the wall, and I see a chart. 'Look on the chart and you will see all the routes with their own, special route number. On each route, you will also see the exact bus that is following that route today. And here,' he pulls a notebook out of his jacket pocket, 'I also keep a pocket version that I make every day, so that I can check for accuracy when I am away from the house. Every time a bus passes me, I can check and confirm that it is the correct vehicle and that my records are accurate.'

He then gives it to me. 'Here, you can have it. I have already made a copy of it for my file, as I knew I was going to give this one to you.' And he gives me a copy of today's bus schedule. Each route is listed, and the name and registration number of the bus is there for me to see.

When I went home that afternoon, I took his copy of the route schedule with me, and I kept it in my drawer for a while. I can still remember some of the detail:

'Leyland PD2 MCW Orion, Vehicle Registration number AFT 930, Route 1A Whitley Bay
Bristol L Single Deck, Vehicle Registration number FT 5705, Route 5 Whitley Bay, St Mary's Island'

Then Hugh says, 'If you want to get a bus back home today, it will be FT 5705 because that is running this afternoon, and that will take you from the bus station in Whitley Bay up through the Marden Estate via the Broadway. AFT 930 sometimes takes the number twelve route, past the Ice Rink and Foxhunters and along to Preston village and into North Shields. It is often better for you to take that and walk down to your house because it is quicker.'

'What's the number of the bus that passes here?' I ask him. 'Number Five,' he replies. 'But you won't need to take that today because my mother has said that she will take you to the bus station.' He has already told me that, and now he is telling me again.

Looking around this room, I am amazed by what I see. Hugh keeps a record of all the journeys that the buses take, and each day he writes out a chart that records what is happening – and he makes a smaller copy to use when he is outside.

'How long have you been doing this, Hugh?'

'Since I was about your age, I think. I have always worked on it. It's a good system now. I keep improving it and it's pretty well up do date. I move the buses along the routes every hour, and I can make the sounds.'

'The sounds?'

'Yes, the engine sounds. Each of these buses has a diesel engine and they all make different sounds. The Cummins is different from the Guy, and the Leyland is different again.'

And he proceeds to demonstrate. He picks up one of his buses from one of his roads, tells me the name of its engine – it is a 'Guy', and then using his lips, he makes a motor sound. He then picks up another bus, tells me this one is a 'Bristol' and does the same thing again. I don't hear any difference in the sounds, but he names the engine before he makes the sound and I nod to him as if I can hear the difference.

All over his model town there are buses travelling on their routes, and Hugh shows me the long stick with a grab-thing on the end that he uses to pick them up – or move them along to where they need to be each hour.

And there is something else that he shows me. 'Do you see the depot on Percy Main?' he asks me. 'Yes.' I reply, 'You mean there, where five or six buses are lined up?' I had noticed this already. They are parked outside the garage that Hugh has built to put the buses in when they finish work. It is quite big, easy to see on the model, and anyway, I know where Percy Main is.

'Some of those buses are in there for maintenance, but one of them is in the Paint Bay.'

He reaches in to the garage and picks up a bus which has been hidden until now. He holds it near my face and he asks me to smell it. I do, and it smells of fresh paint. It has just been painted in the bright red colour that I see on all our buses – except those of Hunter's buses, because those buses are brown. I don't see any Hunter's buses on Hugh's model.

'I went to Percy Main,' he says, 'to the paint bay at the depot, and I asked them if they would let me have a pot of the paint they use for their buses. They said yes – and here it is.'

He points to a big glass jar of red paint. It is about half full.

He explains what he does with the paint. 'The depot paints one bus every week. I do the same. On Monday, Wednesday and Friday, I put a coat of paint, first on the top half of the bus, that's done on Monday. On Wednesday, I do the bottom half and on Friday, I finish off the detail, and I do the number plates. I paint one bus every week, just like they do in the depot, and I paint the exact same bus that they do because I have their painting schedule here.'

And he has! He shows me yet another notebook. In this book, each of the maintenance schedules of each of the buses is listed. Hugh is very proud of all the detail. He knows everything there is to know about the Tynemouth and District bus service.

'You are the only person who has ever seen this,' he says, 'apart from my mother. But I want you to be my special friend, so I have let you see all this.'

I look at him. I don't know what to say. Then I try to make some sense of this. Why am I the only person? What does this mean, 'special friend'? When he explained how he painted the bus, he said more to me then than he had ever spoken before.

Hugh's mother pops her head around the door. 'Would you boys like a cup of tea?' she says. Hugh says yes, but I don't like tea and I ask if I can have a glass of milk. She says of course I can and then she says, 'I am so pleased that Hugh has you for a friend.'

Again – a 'friend'? I hardly know Hugh. He comes to choir practice every few weeks – always when My Haynes can't come - and he mutters. Nobody understands him when he speaks to the choir. He sometimes tries to get us to sing an anthem, but if there are none of the grown-ups, the altos and basses there, the boys just mess about.

Then he gets angry and puts his coat on and sits at the back of the church waiting for his mother to come and pick him up. Never his dad – I don't think he has a dad. His mam is here now, but there is no dad here, and Hugh has never mentioned him.

But I am not his friend. I don't want to be, anyway. I have tried to say hello to him when he comes to choir practice because I am embarrassed that nobody talks to him at all. And once I asked him if he was all right when he went to the back of the church after some of the boys made jokes about him. He looked as if he was crying, but he said that no, he was fine, and would just wait for his mother who should be coming soon.

And on Wednesday, when he asked me after choir practice if I wanted to come here today, his mam had to prod him and remind him. It was embarrassing for me – I did not know what to say, so I said I'll ask my mam, and he then said that two o'clock on Saturday would be fine. And that was it. That was the longest conversation I have ever had with him – until this afternoon, when he started telling me about his buses.

And now he is saying that I am his friend. I am ten years old and he is at least twenty, maybe twenty-five. I can't be his friend, and I don't want to be.

That's it. The end. When I get home tonight, I will tell my mam that I am finishing with the choir because I want to join the Gang Show. I won't mention Hugh Tweed and his model buses, and I won't be taking the Number Five to St Mary's Island ever again.

***

'So how was your visit to your friend?', the first thing Mam says to me when I get home.

'It was all right, I suppose.' I don't know what to think myself, so I can't explain to my mam. Hugh was pleasant, he was kind enough, but there is something strange about him - although I don't want to tell my mam that.

'Where has he been, Mac?' My dad is at home. It is a Saturday and he normally plays the piano on a Saturday.

'He went to meet somebody from the choir – in Whitley Bay.'

'Oh,' says my dad. He has a glass of beer in his hand and he is smiling. 'Did you have a good time? What do choirboys do on a Saturday afternoon? Do you sing hymns?' He laughs and goes to our piano and, without sitting down, he plays a couple of phrases of 'Abide with Me'.

'No,' I reply, 'we played with his buses. He's got this amazing model – it takes up a whole room of his house. There's no space for anything else. It's on two or three tables, it's so big, and it's covered with all the bus routes in North Shields, Whitley Bay and Tynemouth. He knows the times of each bus and even the registration numbers of the buses themselves. He draws up a schedule of bus times every day and when he goes out, he checks every bus that passes by.'

My dad is impressed. 'That sounds very complicated. It must have taken ages. His dad must be a model maker or something. He won't have done it by himself.'

'He hasn't got a dad!' I blurt this out. And then I follow it with, 'At least I don't think so. He did it all himself. He said he started it when he was about ten. It's taken ages for him to do it. It's full of detail. He even paints one bus every week – just like they do with the real buses in the depot.'

My mam looks at me with a strange expression. 'How old is - your friend? How old is Hugh?'

'I don't know exactly. He's a grown up. I think he is over twenty,'

I can't say for sure because all adults look old. Hugh is not a young boy, and one of the reasons why I won't be going back to Whitley Bay is because he is too old. I can't play with somebody of that age, it seems odd – and he is so difficult to talk to.

My mam and dad are looking at each other. Then my dad says, 'This Hugh person, so he's not one of the choirboys, then?'

'No,' I reply, 'he sometimes takes us for choir practice. He's a very good musician. He plays the piano and organ, and he reads music – he's a very interesting man.'

My dad is still staring at my mam. He then says to me, 'Sit down, Anthony.'

I sit, and my mam and dad are still looking at each other. My mam turns to me and says,

'Anthony, when I said that you could go to Hugh Tweed's house, I thought he was another choirboy, and that you were going to play with him.'

'I never said he was a choirboy, Mam ...'

'And he's not a bloody choirboy is he, Mac?' My dad is now looking angrily at my mam. 'Did you not think to ask? He's spent the afternoon with a bloke.' Then, to me, 'Did that man do anything to you, Anthony?'

'What do you mean, Dad?'

'Did that man touch you at all?' Then my mam adds, 'Did he try to – kiss you, or give you a cuddle?'

'What? No! We just looked at his buses and at the timetables. He gave me a copy of one of his schedules. His mam made us a drink and then she drove me to the bus station and I came home.'

I take out of my pocket the schedule for today that Hugh has given me, and I hold it so that my dad can see it. 'He makes one of these every day.'

My dad takes the schedule, and glances at it. 'Did that man try to touch you in any way at all?'

'No Dad, he didn't. He's a nice man. He's very shy and he doesn't talk to many people. But he is kind – and he is very clever.'

'He might be clever, Anthony. But grown up men don't take little boys to their houses.'

'I'm not going back,' I say. 'Model buses don't interest me.'

'Model buses don't interest you?' My dad is blustering, 'Let me tell you something, young man. If you ever even think of seeing that Hugh man again, I'll bloody well swing for you.'

I know what that means. It means that he is very angry with me. My mam uses the same words when she is very angry too.

'What's more,' he continues, 'you can forget the choir. Choir is over – finished. You are not going back there again. I'll write a letter to the vicar explaining.'

My mam says, 'Stan, you can't go accusing ...'

'I'm not accusing anybody - yet! However, Anthony is leaving the choir – as of now. I will ask about this bloke at the Whitley Bay club, and if I do find out that anybody has been molesting my son, there'll be hell to pay!'

He then turns to me, 'Go to your room, Anthony. Your mother and I have some things to talk about.'

There has been some shouting downstairs, and my dad has just left the house, slamming the door loudly.

From my bedroom window, I look over in to the back garden of our house and into the windows of the new houses behind us. I am thinking about Hugh Tweed. I don't understand what all the fuss was about. Hugh did not make me feel frightened at all. I think that I feel sorry for him. I know that he finds it very difficult to talk to anyone – even to me, and he says I am his friend.

I won't go back to his house. I'm not interested in his models and his bus routes. That's the only reason I won't go back.

But what did my dad say about not going back to the choir again? And I didn't even have to ask if I could leave. My mam and dad have made the decision for me. Next week, I'll start rehearsals for the Gang Show.

Nine
Gangs and Gang Shows

To enter a theatre for a performance is to be inducted into a magical space, to be ushered into the sacred arena of the imagination. Simon Callow

Mr Brandreth has agreed to take me and his son Michael to the first Gang Show rehearsal. It is a Tuesday night, and it is raining. The rehearsal is to start at seven o'clock, and Mr Carr, our Akela, has decided to come as well. We both walk round to Mr Brandreth's house at six thirty.

Mr Brandreth is standing by his car when we arrive. He is polishing the bonnet of his white Vauxhall Velox. It is quite a new car, and I have never been this close to it before. There is no sign of Michael.

'Just tonight for me, Jack,' says Akela. 'If it's all right with you, I'll pinch a lift with Anthony. Later on, I'll be doing the lights for the show, but I just want to be there for the first meeting. See how things go.'

'No, that's fine,' says Mr Brandreth. 'Here,' and he opens the door, 'Get in – you in the front, Reg, Anthony – you get in the back.' As Akela opens the door to get in the car, Mr Brandreth says, 'Our Michael loved the Gang Show last year.' He then lowers his voice and still talking to Akela, says 'So I want him to do it again. Anything to keep him away from those lads up the street.'

I don't know Michael very well. He's two years older than I am and he goes to Linskill school. That means that he didn't pass the eleven plus. In a way, I am quite surprised that Michael is a scout – not that the eleven plus has anything to do with that, but because whenever I see him, he seems always to be with a gang of tough boys from further up the street.

I know that these boys smoke, and I have seen Michael smoking too. They hang around the hut at the top of the field that is called the Community Centre, and I heard my dad saying that there had been some trouble up there a few days ago. Some old ladies had been called names when they left the hut, and Michael and the other boys were blamed.

My dad knows this, and he said that he wasn't too happy about me going to the rehearsals with Michael, but my mam said that as long as Mr Brandreth and Akela were going, there was nothing to worry about.

My dad agreed: well, he didn't exactly agree. He's been very angry about a visit I made a little while ago to Whitley Bay to see that Hugh

Tweed, and he thought it would be best if my mam went with me to the rehearsals. My mam said no, that it was a bad idea, and anyway, Reg Carr was going with me, and there's nothing wrong with Reg Carr, is there? Also, it means that there was no bus fare to worry about either.

We're in the car now, and still waiting for Michael. Mr Brandreth peeps the horn and after maybe two more minutes, Michael appears.

Akela is in the front seat and Mr Brandreth is driving. That means that Michael is to get in the back, where I am already sitting. This seems to make him annoyed, and as he gets into the car to sit behind Akela, he slams his body into the back seat, totally ignoring me.

'Are you all right there, Michael?' asks Akela. I wonder if he is worried about sitting in the front and if Michael maybe expects to be sitting there. Michael says nothing.

'Don't worry about him, Reg,' says Michael's dad. 'He'll sit where I tell him to sit.'

I look over towards Michael. I want to smile and say hello – just polite really, but as I do so, he reaches his hand towards my knee, and he presses his thumb as hard as he can, into that soft part just above my kneecap.

I make a noise, half a scream, half surprise, and Akela turns around to me and says, 'Is everything all right, Tony?'

'I just bashed my knee as I moved to make way for Michael,' I say. 'I'm ok now.'

Michael looks at me and smiles but is not a friendly smile. He's sitting very low in the car and I don't think that his dad can see him in the mirror. My knee hurts.

'Right, let's get going.' And Mr Brandreth pulls out into Hartington Road and begins to drive us to North Shields.

As we turn into Hartburn Road, we all see three of the boys that Michael now plays with. They are the tough boys on the estate. I keep away from them, but sometimes about ten or more of them hang about together, and there are girls too. One of the boys has a girlfriend, and she is always with him.

The boys have seen Michael's car, and as we drive past them, they are laughing – I think they are laughing at Michael. Michael certainly thinks this because he reaches out to me again as if he was going to grab my knee, but his dad says, 'Michael, why were those boys laughing at you?' Michael stops, folds his arms but says nothing.

'Michael, I asked you a question.'

'What?' says Michael.

'What were those boys laughing at?'

'Me. They were laughing at me. They know I'm going to sing stupid songs with soft kids.'

'I thought you liked the scouts, Michael,' says his dad. 'You like going to camp, don't you? And it was you who said you wanted to be in the Gang Show again.'

'That was last year – I was a kid then!' Michael doesn't speak this so much as sneer it. And his dad is embarrassed. He apologises to Akela.

'And you are such a big man now, aren't you?' Michael's dad sneers back at his son.

Akela says, 'Don't worry, Jack. He's a young man now. Growing up is difficult nowadays. They all want to grow up so quickly.'

Michael is picking away at a seam on the back of Akela's seat. It comes away and he starts to undo it.

'You're too big for the scouts, is that it, Michael? You'd prefer to hang around with teddy boys and get yourself into trouble? So, if we don't go to the first rehearsal, that will be all right with you, then. Will it?'

No answer: 'Michael, I am talking to you. Will it be all right if we don't go?'

Michael shrugs his shoulders and looks out of the window. This is becoming embarrassing.

'Well, Michael?'

'Well what? I don't care! Do whatever you want to do. You always do!'

'Fine!' replies his dad. 'But, if you are giving backword – breaking your promise - you are going to go into that hall yourself, and you will apologise to the man who invited you to return this year. There are other kids who deserved your place but didn't get the chance - so you've let them down too.'

'You can tell him. This was your idea, not mine. I'm not going in there. I'm staying in the car!' Michael has obviously decided that the Gang Show is not for him. I am embarrassed and thinking that I should not be here, and I am sure that Akela feels the same way.

We drive in total silence for about five more minutes until we arrive at Christ Church hall, and Mr Brandreth pulls up. There are traffic lights right outside the hall, so he drives on to the pavement so that other cars can pass by.

'Right, Reg, here we are – and you, Anthony, you can get out at my side.'

I say thank you to Mr Brandreth who doesn't pay either me or Akela much attention. He has walked around to the passenger side of the car and has leaned into the back. Michael comes stumbling out of the car as Mr Brandreth pulls him.

'Leave off. I'm not going in there.' Michael tries to break free, but his dad hangs on to him.

'I think you'll find that you are. You can do this the easy way, or you can do it the hard way. The easy way is when you go into the hall, seek out Mr Bradbeer and apologise to him for letting everybody down, and you tell him that you won't be able to join the Gang Show this year.

'The hard way is when you do the same thing, but I drag you in to the hall to make you do it. Now, which do you choose?'

Mr Brandreth is very angry. I know which I would choose. Akela has gone off into the hall. He did say goodbye and thank you to Mr Brandreth, but I don't think that Mr Brandreth heard.

'Which is it?' Mr Brandreth repeats the offer.

'The easy way,' mutters Michael.

'Speak up, boy. What did you say?'

'I said the easy way - now leave off me.' And Michael pulls himself away from his dad's grip. As he does so, he catches my eye and looks at me. He doesn't say anything, but I know exactly what he means. He needs somebody to blame, and he has chosen me.

This is so unfair. I've done nothing wrong, and it was Akela who arranged the lift, not me.

I go into the hall and up the stairs by myself, and when I get through the door, I see that Akela is talking to a man who has a clipboard in his hand and a pen, and Akela points me out to him.

'Ah yes. Tony, isn't it?' he says, looking at me. 'This way, young man. I'm pleased that you have come.'

I say hello to the man who Michael's dad mentioned in the car, and Mr Bradbeer introduces himself, says that he will be helping to produce the Gang Show, and he ticks my name off on a list. He is wearing scout uniform, and I think that I have seen him before.

'Welcome back young Tony. I heard you singing at the auditions – that day that Ted Potts was with us, remember?'

I remember him now. He was in scout uniform then too and was with a group of other men. 'Go and sit over there, and we'll get started when everybody has arrived,' he says.

I sit down on a chair and look around the room. There are maybe twenty boys there, some sitting alone, some standing and chatting, some laughing at something, and they all look older than me.

About six or seven of the boys are wearing scout uniform, there are four boys over at the other side of the room wearing their school clothes, and one or two are wearing jeans.

I notice one boy wearing a new pair of 'Varlson Wranglers' – those are the jeans I really want - he has turned them up three inches, just as I would do – and he has luminous lime green socks too. I think that he looks great!

Michael Brandreth comes in with his dad. I think he has chosen the 'easy option' because his dad is a step or two ahead him, but not dragging him in like he said that he would. Michael has his hands in his pockets and his head is hunched into his shoulders.

He shuffles over to where Mr Bradbeer is standing. As Michael passes his dad, Mr Brandreth whispers quietly to his son, and he removes his hands from his pockets. Mr Bradbeer turns towards Michael.

I can't hear a word they are saying, but I can tell – we all can tell – that Michael is very embarrassed. He is blushing, his head is lowered, and his shoulders are slumped. All conversations in the room have stopped, and everyone is watching what is happening between a very unhappy looking Michael Brandreth and Mr Bradbeer.

Mr Bradbeer has just asked him a question. I can see that he repeats the question as Michael seems not to have heard. Then Michael shrugs: that is his answer; his dad moves forward, shakes Mr Bradbeer's hand and says something to his son. Michael turns, puts his hands in his pockets and walks out of the room – still with his head down and not looking at anyone.

Mr Brandreth then moves towards Akela and says a few words to him. I can't make out what they are saying, but I bet he is telling Akela that he and I must find our own way back home tonight.

The rehearsal begins. I am only a wolf cub; I am not a scout. Although I do have my Leaping Wolf, and my cub uniform is covered with badges, I am still too young to be a scout. I am also feeling quite nervous when I look around, as I appear to be the youngest person in the room.

Akela comes to sit beside me. 'Don't worry about your lift home, Tony,' he says, 'I'll work something out with Phil before the next rehearsal, but tonight, we'll get the bus back.'

It's not the lift that I am worried about, but Akela is right, I am worried. I am worried about what Michael Brandreth is going to do to me when he gets the chance. He was very angry, and when he had to go and explain himself to Phil Bradbeer, I could see how embarrassed he was.

I know that he will blame me for this – even though it is nothing to do with me – and I know that somehow, he will take it out on me. I am sure of that, because that's what he and those big boys do.

My first ever Gang Show rehearsal goes very quickly – it's all a bit of a blur because although I want to concentrate on the script and the songs, I keep on thinking about Michael Brandreth and the way he looked at me. And I am scared, really scared.

After the rehearsal, I go home with Akela on the number twelve, and he tells me that I have done very well.

'Phil thinks that there are two, possibly three songs that you could do, not including the chorus songs. In one of them, you might be singing with another boy, and there is a very funny sketch which has five boys in it, and Phil thinks that might be suitable too. So, well done, Tony.'

'Thanks,' I reply. 'I enjoyed it. It's much more fun than going to choir.'

'Good', replies Akela, 'I think it will suit you perfectly. You get to have a laugh, but one thing about the Gang Show is that it builds your confidence – and it makes you friends too. I just wish that our Reg was interested. Now that you are going, I'll see if I can get him to join again. He tried it; didn't like it at all.'

Akela says that being in the Gang Show will build my confidence? If only it would. How I am going to be able to keep away from Michael – because I know, I just know that he will come after me? I wonder if I should mention this to Akela now, but I decide not to. It's not his problem, it's mine. And maybe I am wrong, maybe Michael does not intend to come after me, and I am just frightening myself.

But how I am going to be able to get to rehearsals, now that Michael Brandreth's dad won't be coming to pick me up?

***

I am still going to rehearsals! Akela fixed it for me. Chris Johnstone has just joined the Gang Show as well – I didn't see him, but he says he was there on the night that Michael Brandreth decided not to take part, but he only came to put his name down. He had to leave after a few minutes. He goes every week now, though.

Chris lives on The Broadway, and his mam is taking him to rehearsals in her car and bringing him back. My house is on the way, so Akela asked Mrs Johnstone if she minded taking me to rehearsals as well, and she said she was happy to. She also offered to take Reg Carr's son too, but he said no, he was quite happy playing football – and his training was on the same nights as our rehearsals.

I know Chris Johnstone well. I was in the Infants with him at Cullercoats school before I moved to Monkhouse primary. I was playing with him one lunch time when he had his eye put out by a boy who had brought a bow and arrow to school. I remember his teacher holding a hankie over his eye and cuddling him at the same time.

Chris had to have a glass eye. The arrow had blinded him in one eye and our head teacher banned all bows and arrows. The Davey Crockett craze ended soon after, but while it was on, I always took my six–gun to school because I wasn't an Indian – I was a cowboy. Some boys who were Indians were quite annoyed, but when Chris was blinded, they stopped.

Having a glass eye doesn't stop Chris doing things. He takes part in everything; he loves playing football and running around. We have a great time together at rehearsals because we both like singing, and although we thought that the dancing was a bit silly to begin with, we are starting to enjoy that too – not that we can do it.

I have a list of the numbers that I am taking part in, and I have made a separate list for each half of the show. Phil Bradbeer calls it the 'running order'.

In the first half, I am in the chorus for 'Crest of a Wave', then the third number is called 'Love Love'. It sounds a bit soppy, but it is not. Three boys sing it, and I am one of them. We each have a verse, and we sing the chorus together.

Then I am in two chorus numbers: 'Meet the Navy' and 'Red, White and Blue'. For each of these numbers I have a change of costume, and I was also told that we will have to put on stage make-up too. I wore stage make-up when I was in the nativity play last year, and I know how to mix 'five' and 'nine' already – and all about the carmine 'dot'.

In the second half of the show I might have a solo. It is called 'It's a Beautiful Thing to Go Nowhere' and Phil tells me that I will be on stage all by myself.

I am also in the last chorus number of the show, the Finale, which is called 'Jamboree'. Phil tells us all that for this special number we will we using 'ultra violet light' which will make all our costumes – and our teeth - shine brightly. He promised that Reg Carr will demonstrate this ultra violet light to us during one of the rehearsals.

I know about this special kind of lighting because my Uncle John in Wallsend Road has an ultra violet lamp. He calls it his 'health' lamp. I saw it switched on once. Uncle John has false teeth and when he smiled, his teeth shone brightly. I am excited about how the stage will look when forty boys are all smiling at the same time.

I am very happy and surprised that I have so much to do in my first Gang Show. I practise my songs every night in front of the mirror, and I really look forward to each rehearsal.

It was a big surprise when Mr Bradbeer asked me to sing a solo. He says that I will have to audition again, and I must go to an address in Whitley Bay which is where the musical director lives. When he picks me up, Phil says that we are going to see the musical director because he has the last word for the solos in all the Gang Shows.

The musical director is the man I first met – I could never forget that moustache. It is still all curled up at the ends. This is Mr William Watson Todd, and this is his house.

As soon as I arrive, I see why Mr Bradbeer has asked me to go there. We go in to the front room of the house, and in it is a huge Hammond organ – that's the reason. We only use a piano for rehearsals, and Phil explains to me that they want to find out if my voice will be strong enough to sing over the sound of the band.

Mr Todd, Phil calls him 'Watson', is very kind, and when he sits down and begins to play, the sound of the organ is like an orchestra.

'Now then, Tony,' I want you to be able to sing this song, and if it works out well, we'll ask Gillian if she can work out some dance steps for you,'

I have watched Gillian working in rehearsal. She is the only female I have seen at rehearsal – except for the mams that bring their boys and take them home. She shows everybody the steps for their numbers. Mr Todd seems to want me to dance as well as sing.

He begins to play, and I try my best to sing the song, but I just can't get it. I am nervous, I know, but the harder I try, the worse it becomes. Mr Todd says that he will arrange it in a different key, but that just seems to make things worse. The problem is that I can't reach the high notes.

When I leave Mr Todd's house, he is very polite, but I think that he is disappointed.

In the car, Mr Bradbeer says not to worry. It's because I am a 'treble', he says. Apparently both he and Mr Todd thought that I might be a 'boy soprano'. But I am not.

'Richard Bamford has a soprano voice, and we thought that if we had two sopranos, that solo would work for you, and he could have the other.'

I have heard Richard Bamford sing. He is also a wolf cub, but he is from another pack. His voice is very high, and I have tried to reach the notes he sings in rehearsal, but I know that I can't.

'I am sorry,' I say. I am not sure what to be sorry about, but I know that I have let them both down. They expected something, or they would not have spent all this time and effort with me.

'No.' Mr Bradbeer turns from looking at the road and looks at me. 'Nothing to be sorry about. You've got a good treble voice, Tony, and we will use that. There aren't that many good boy sopranos about, that's all. You have a good ear, and you can hold a note well, so I thought it was worth the try. You'll be great in the other numbers, I know that.'

And he drops me off at home, says goodbye and drives off.

'How was the audition, Anthony?' My mam has heard the car pull up, and she opens the door just as Mr Bradbeer drives off. My mam waves, but I don't think that he notices her.

'It was ok,' I lie. 'They were thinking of introducing new song and asked me to sing it.'

'That's wonderful, my pet.' They must think that you are talented.'

When did you start lying to your parents? Here am I, just coming up to ten years of age, and I am a practised liar. I don't want to tell my mam that I failed the audition, and that Richard Bamford is going to sing the song that I was supposed to sing. She will tell my dad, and he will come out with all his 'tin ear' jokes again – and I don't want that.

'I hope that I get it,' I continue. 'It is a good song, but they aren't sure if it is going to fit into the production.'

'But they have asked you to sing it, that's the important thing.'

It is true that they have asked me to sing it. So, I leave it at that, and go to the kitchen to make myself something to eat. There's nothing in the pantry except my mam's Energen Rolls. These look like bread buns, but they taste like nothing at all – like cotton wool, I suppose. I can put a whole one in my mouth and it melts away in a second. There is some margarine there too.

I put one of the Energen Rolls into my mouth, then I cut open three more, and spread some margarine on to them. I make my way upstairs to my bedroom while my mother sits in her chair, feet and legs close to the fire, while she smokes her 'Player's Navy Cut' cigarette and reads her library book.

***

And Michael Brandreth does get me! He found me when I had to go to the clinic. I have eczema on my arms and legs, and sometimes it flares up. If I touch a dog or a cat, for example, I know that I must wash my hands immediately or my eczema will get worse.

However, there seem to be other things that make it flare up as well. If I worry, or if I get nervous, I sometimes scratch myself all night, and when I wake up, the back of my legs or my wrists and elbows are red raw where I have been scratching. Then my mam takes me to the doctor's, but today she told me to go by myself to the clinic at the community centre.

The community centre is just around the corner from where Michael lives. To get to it, I would normally walk right past his house because it is on my way, but today I deliberately take the slightly longer way up Wallington Avenue, to avoid seeing him.

It does not work! The nurse in the clinic wants to take off all my bandages and put on some new ones, and she also gives me a big tub of ointment to put on my scabs at night. I am in the clinic, first waiting for my turn, and then seeing the nurse, for almost half an hour.

When I come out from the clinic, Michael is waiting for me. He is with Clifford and Henry, two of the big boys from up the road. They are in the gang that causes all the trouble around here.

I should go back in to the clinic, but I decide to walk past them. They let me go past, and then Michael says, 'Sing us a song, little boy,' and his friends laugh.

I walk on, I really want to run away as fast as I can, but I know that Michael Brandreth is a very fast runner, and he would easily catch me.

The three of them begin to follow me. They are very close, and Michael puts out his foot in front of me to try to trip me up. I stumble, but I do not fall. I continue to walk, but Michael has waited long enough. He runs in front of me, turns and stops, so I have to stop too.

'You got me into trouble, you scabby little twat!'

'No, I didn't! It was nothing to do with me.'

'My dad was angry – and it was all because of you. You and those stupid scouts!'

Then he hits me. He punches me in the stomach and winds me. The tub of ointment spills out of my hands. 'That's for making my dad angry!' He punches me again – this time on the back of my head because I am doubled up, 'And that's for being a scabby singing fairy!'

He and his friends run off laughing. I sit on a wall trying to get my breath. Janet Larty comes out of her house and sees me.

'Anthony.' she says as she come towards me – seeing the three boys now punching each other and laughing as they make their way up the street. 'Are you all right? Did those boys hurt you?'

'No,' I reply, 'It was a – misunderstanding. It was a mistake. I am ok.' I am not ok, I am hurt, and I want to cry. Janet Larty is in a class above me, and I don't want her to see me crying.

This is terrible! I have dropped my tub of ointment on the floor. The tub is made of a kind of waxed cardboard, and when I dropped it, the lid fell off, and some of the ointment is in the gutter. I am going to get into trouble for that too when I get home.

Janet has seen the tub too. She bends down and picks it up for me. She is able to re-shape the tub so that the lid fits on to it properly. She has left the spilled ointment in the gutter where it has landed. I wipe the edges of the tub with my hands and now it doesn't look as if it has been dropped.

'If those boys have been bullying you,' continues Janet, 'you should tell somebody. They cause a lot of trouble on the estate, they are always in trouble.'

'I can't do that. You know I can't do that. It will only make things worse.'

I suppose it's easy for her to say that, but Janet just doesn't understand. She is the same as the grown-ups when this kind of thing happens. She thinks that when I tell somebody like my dad or my head teacher, they will do something about it. Yes, they will. But the problem won't go away. The boys will find out and then they will always be after me. I don't want to worry that Michael Brandreth is going to be seeking his revenge.

When I get home, I put the tub of ointment down on the kitchen table, and I go out into the back garden to mooch around in the weeds and long grass and think. My mam is out down the shops. I am looking around; my mind is not focused on anything, but I am trying to make some sense of what is going on.

I am not worried about what Michael – or anyone else – thinks about my songs in the Gang Show. This is the best thing I have ever done – so much more interesting than the choir – so I won't stop going to rehearsals.

But the Michael Brandreth bullying thing is different. I don't know what to do, but I feel that I must do something. Those boys frighten me, they are older and bigger than I am – and there are three of them. I can't fight any of them. I couldn't even fight one of them.

I step into the wash house by the kitchen door and I poke around in the huge pile of rubbish, full of things that have been dumped in there because they are 'spare' or because my dad has kept them 'just in case'.

I see my dad's old army uniform, which is still hanging on the same hook years after I gave it to a rag and bone man for a shilling. My dad came back home, and he went crazy when he found out what I had done. He went out looking for the man and brought his uniform back. It is still there after all this time. Next to it, I see an old tin of paint, and the memory of what I did with that paint all comes back to me.

That tin of paint has stayed in our wash house, unused, from when I was a little boy. I was maybe four or five years old when it got me into a lot of trouble because we used it to decorate the gates and gateposts of our houses. We wanted to please our parents, but they got very angry with us instead. And it was that tin of grey undercoat that we used.

I have decided what I will do. It won't be today, but very soon Michael, Clifford and Henry will see their names painted up on the door of the community centre. First, I thought about painting their names on Mr Brandreth's white Vauxhall Velox, but I decided not this time, but if Michael bullies me again, I will know what to do about it.

Ten

My Faith Healer and a Lobster

'I've learned that sometimes a smile represents the greatest form of deceit.'
Michael Gilbert

My dad comes home from the match – I think he has also been to the pub on the way home. It is about eight o'clock on a Saturday. He's late if he's going out to play the piano at his club tonight, so he will be in a rush. But he's not rushing. He wants a word with me and Mam. As he walks into the front room, he is already talking, 'This eczema, Mac. Anthony's eczema – you know, the rashes and all that?'

'What about it?' My mam isn't very happy. I know she expected Dad to be home earlier. He went out this morning and didn't come back. He was going to take me to the football match at Appleby Park this afternoon, but he must have forgotten. My dad sometimes writes for the 'Pink – un', the sports newspaper, on a Saturday; he reports on our team, North Shields, and he takes me to some of the matches.

'Did you forget about Anthony?'

'What? I'm talking about Anthony now – you just heard me.'

'Yes,' Mam replies – quite quickly. She is annoyed about something. 'Now you are talking about him. I said have you forgotten about him?

'What do you mean?'

'You said you would be taking Anthony to the match with you. You were popping round to Jimmy Ferguson's and then you were coming straight back. But you didn't come, and Anthony has been waiting around all day.'

'I'm sorry, Son.' That's the first time he's looked at me. 'I forgot. Jimmy said he would give me a lift to the ground, and I didn't think. I just got into Jimmy's van.'

'It's ok, Dad,' I say, 'I went out to play with Ian.'

I did. I got bored playing with Glenda, my sister. She's still playing with dollies on the floor and smiling at my dad, but he hasn't seen her.

My mam interrupts, 'It's not ok, Anthony. It's certainly not ok. Stan, you broke a promise and disappointed your son – and you've been to the pub as well.'

'I only had one pint, Mac.'

'Oh yes?' My mam does not believe him. 'And the rest. And I suppose that now you'll be off playing the piano and forgetting us all.'

'No no no!' my dad continues. 'I'm not working tonight. Let me get this coat off first. What I am trying to say is – just give me a moment and you will understand.'

He takes off the raincoat that he always wears. It has a belt around the waist and he seems to have some trouble undoing it. I think that my mam is right. He has been drinking – and more than he says he has.

He moves to sit down, draping his coat over the back of the chair, and he lights one of his Woodbines. He seems a little more settled now.

'I had a chat with a man today.'

'I can tell.' My mam is still annoyed, and seeing the trouble he had lighting his cigarette, she now knows that he has been in the pub.

'Just listen, will you, please. I was in the Spread Eagle.' The Spread Eagle is a pub in Preston village. Dad often goes there. 'I stopped off on my way back home.' The landlord, Charlie Went, is a friend of dad's. Mrs Went came on holiday with us when we went to Osmotherley.

I can tell that my mam is still really angry with Dad. I don't often see her like this. She opens her packet of cigarettes – she always smokes Players - and she takes one out, lights it, and she breathes out the smoke in that special way that shows that she is really annoyed.

'Mac. Just listen, for heaven's sake! I've said that I am sorry that I forgot about Anthony and the match – I'll take him next week. We're playing away at West Sleekburn, and we'll make a day of it, I promise that I'll not forget him this time. But this is what I want to tell you. I've been talking about Anthony all afternoon.'

'I went to the Spread Eagle to phone in my copy for tonight's paper, and I was just about to come home when I met this man at the bar. He's a friend of Charlie's – it was Charlie who introduced him to me, and he thinks he might be able to help Anthony with his eczema.'

'He's a doctor?' I think that my mam is surprised that Charlie Went has a friend who is a doctor.

'No – it's better than that. He's not a doctor, he's a faith healer.'

'A what?' My mam is puzzled. In my head, I have just asked the same question.

'Yes, he's a faith healer. He told Charlie and me that he has a 'gift'. He can make people well again. It seems that he does this all over the North East. We got chatting and I mentioned Anthony and the problem he has with the eczema on his arms and legs. He said he could help him.'

My mam turns to my dad. She still angry, but I see that she is calming down, 'How can he help? What does he do, this faith healer?'

'He heals people. I don't know what he does, exactly, but he says he can heal Anthony.' My dad looks at me, then at my mam. It's as if I'm not there when he says to Mam, 'His skin looks awful most of the time. All those bandages, and all that cream stuff that you've got to put on him every night. Anything is worth trying, isn't it?

'I think that there will be some praying, I suppose. But you don't mind that, do you Son? You pray often enough at church – in the choir. It will be just like the prayers in church, but here – at home.'

My mam looks at me and says, 'Anthony, what do you think, pet?'

I don't know what to think. I just shrug. I hate the prayers at church. I always think of other things because I can't understand the idea of talking to God. I hate the prayers, but the sermons are even worse. The vicar goes on and on, and I lose interest so quickly. Mostly I play noughts and crosses with the boy next to me. We did try 'church cricket once, but David Haynes shouted 'Howzat.' and his dad – who is the choirmaster – banned us from ever playing it again.

'I think that we should try anything that will help you,' my dad says, 'So, he's coming around tomorrow afternoon at four o'clock. Anthony, make sure that you have a bath.'

'Is this man going to cost money?' My mam is worried. 'If it's going to cost money, you should have asked me first, Stan. Things are tight enough at the moment – you know that – without adding faith healers to our bills.' The way she says 'faith healers' tells me that she has not much faith in this idea.

'It's not a lot of money, more a - contribution, that's what he called it. Yes, a contribution. I've already paid him for tomorrow, so let's see how it goes.'

'How much did you pay him?'

'Not in front of the boy, Mac. I'll tell you later.'

Mam and Dad now start speaking to each other in what they call 'French'. It's a language that they started to use together when I first began speaking. They use it now when they don't want me and Glenda to know what they are talking about. It's English really, but they pronounce the words in a silly, foreign way, so that we don't understand them – and they think they fool us in this way, and maybe they do fool Glenda, but they don't fool me any longer.

My dad has paid three pounds for the man to come tomorrow. I know that he earns just over eleven pounds a week in his main job as a clerical officer in Longbenton. In this language of theirs, this amount sounds like 'threeseee poundseeee????', and my mam has just asked that question.

My dad's reply comes in the same stupid, whining voice that my mam has just used. It's more like the Goon Show or a chinaman singing than a French person speaking, but they persist with it. I don't mind. I understand every word they are saying, so I get the whole picture.

'He willee come eachee weekee untilee it worksee. But he willee onlyee charge twoee poundsee afteree tomorrowee.'

I just want to put them out of their misery! This is embarrassing enough for me and I am only ten years old. It must be excruciating for them to carry on like this. And I am sure they both know that I understand exactly what they are saying.

They stop speaking in 'French', and I am pleased to see that they are both smiling – a bit. My mam is still prickly, and still angry that my dad has paid some money to a 'faith healer.' She asks when did he start having faith in faith healers, and I think that is quite funny.

Dad smiles too, sits at the piano and begins to play a Max Bygraves' song 'Meet me on the Corner'. He plays songs like this most nights at the club. My mam gets up to make him tea because he's not going out to work tonight, and I sit down on the floor with my little sister, Glenda, and knock over some of the houses that she has been quietly building for her dolls to live in.

She should be in bed soon, and my mam suddenly realises that and comes out of the kitchen telling my dad to keep an eye on the stove while she puts Glenda to bed. My dad nods and I think he hears, but when the pan boils over, I have to tell him so that he can stop playing the piano and get up and turn off the stove.

After Dad has finished his tea, he tells us that he 'has to see a man about a dog' and he puts his coat on and goes. He tells Mam that he won't be late because he is working for Jimmy Ferguson tomorrow and then to me he says, would I like to help him?

Sometimes my dad does weekend milk deliveries for Jimmy Ferguson to earn a little extra cash – he does this as well as his day job up at Longbenton, his piano playing at night and his Saturday afternoon sports reporting. I don't see much of him at home, but quite often, he wakes me up very early on a Saturday or Sunday morning and takes me with him on the milk round.

Then, I sit next to him in the front seat of the freezing cold van as we drive, first to Jimmy's cold store to load up the milk, the eggs, the orange juice and the cream, and then we are off to the houses, hotels and restaurants in Whitley Bay or Tynemouth.

Just before we arrive at the first drop off point, my dad stops the van, opens the doors at the back and secures them so that they do not slam. Then I get out of my seat at the front, sit on the floor of back of the van, the rear doors being secured open, and my dad drives up to the first house on his list. He barks out the order, and I carry it to the door or the gate, deliver the milk, pick up the empties, chuck them into the empty crates and leap back on to the van as my dad moves to the next stop.

(By the way, not only do I learn how to carry three or four bottles of milk at the same time, but I also discover that empty spirits and wine bottles, left outside the back of the pubs and hotels, often contain just enough to offer an interesting taste sensation to a very immature palate. I wonder how many kids of ten could express a preference for Benedictine? I could.)

My dad only gets me to go out with him every now and again. If he can be bothered, I guess. I might make his delivery job a little easier, but on the other hand, he has to wake me up and then wait for me to get dressed – and my mam always tries to make me have a hot drink before I go out, so if he is in a rush, he just gets up and goes.

Today we finish our milk round at about half past eight, and instead of going straight back to the cold store as we usually do, getting ready for tomorrow by stacking the crates of empty bottles and hosing down the inside of the van, we drive down to the Fish Quay.

I love this place. I love to see the trawlers and the drifters all tied up, the fishermen busily offloading their catches. My dad knows many of the men on the quay here, and after a few minutes, he has collected a couple of bags of fresh fish to take home. In the bags, he tells me there is cod, whiting, some other fish that he doesn't know the name of, and a special treat for my mam in a separate bag – Dad says it is a lobster.

'This will make your mam happy, Son,' he says, 'She will love the lobster.' And he gives me one of the bags to hold.

Yes, I think that this will make her very happy. She loves fish, and crab, mussels – I think she likes all seafood. I only like white fish like cod, but there's a new kind of fish you can get now called 'fish fingers', and I have had one of those. Stephen Robson's dad works in a grocery shop that sells them frozen in packets, and he brought some home one night when I was playing with Stephen.

He cooked one for each of us. Fish fingers are delicious. Much nicer than real fish – and no bones to worry about. You need a refrigerator at home if you are going to buy fish fingers, and we don't have one.

The bag I am holding moves. I drop it quickly and jump away from it. My dad laughs. 'That's the lobster, Son. It's still alive. We'll boil it when we get home. That's the way you kill them.'

Did anybody see me when I jumped? I look around to check. No, I have no need to feel embarrassed. The Fish Quay is a very busy place at this time of the morning, and I always like going there. There are loads of small stalls lined up right along the road, full of all sorts of seafood – and it's all really fresh.

The auction is happening now in the covered area and you can hear the auctioneer's high-pitched voice selling crate after crate of fish. I thought that my parents' 'French' was weird; it makes a lot of sense when compared to the language that the auctioneer uses – I don't understand a word he says.

Dad and I carry our fish to the van and get in to make our way back to the cold store. He lets me have a carton of fresh orange juice as my treat, and after we park the milk van and walk up home carrying not only our fresh fish but also some milk and some orange juice – and gill of cream. It is about ten o'clock.

We get home and give my mam the fish. She sees the lobster moving and smiles at my dad. She says, 'We'll have that tonight, Stan. Bring a bottle of beer home and we'll enjoy it together.'

Then she picks up the bag with the lobster in it and puts it in the kitchen sink. 'He'll be safe there,' she says, 'we don't want him wandering, do we?' She puts the rest of the fish that dad has brought into the larder and says, 'I'll ask Norah if we can put all this fish in her fridge. It'll go off if we leave it in the larder. What time do you want to eat?'

'I won't be here, Mac,' my dad says. 'Sorry. I'm playing at the Crescent Club in Cullercoats this afternoon, and I am at Rosehill in Wallsend tonight. I won't finish there until gone ten, and I'm at work tomorrow. I'll stay at Winlaton Mill with Benny and Joyce.'

Joyce works in the same office as my dad, and her husband, Benny, has a car. He takes Joyce in to work every day, so Dad will also get a lift in. My dad likes Joyce. I know that because he has a photo of her in his wallet – I have seen it.

My mam frowns and then says, 'All right, Stan. Anthony and I will enjoy the lobster tonight, won't we pet?'

I'm not sure that I will enjoy the lobster. It's been looking at me from the sink where we have put it. It is trying to get out. Its claws are made safe with rubber bands around them, but I don't fancy touching it. I am sure that it would be able to get me somehow.

'Don't forget Mr Armstrong – Archie,' says my dad. He's coming at four.'

You should be here to see him, Stan,' snaps my mother. 'You invited him.'

'Yes, but not to see me. He's coming to see Anthony and you'll be there son, won't you?'

I am still thinking about the lobster, not about this faith healer man, and I don't reply.

'Anthony. I was speaking to you!'

'Leave him alone, Stan. He's nervous. Can't you see that?'

Yes, I am nervous, but it's the lobster that's making me nervous. Dad said you had to boil it to kill it. That's cruel, isn't it? I am thinking of what it must be like to be boiled.

'As long as he is here at four o'clock. I've paid him already, so I don't want the money wasted. Now, just time for forty winks. I was up too early this morning. Wake me up at one.' And off he goes to bed.

***

Mr Armstrong, the faith healer, arrives. It is twenty past four, and he apologises to my mam and explains that the bus was late.

I look at him. He is older than my dad, and his head is bald – no hair at all. He has no eyebrows either. He is wearing a black suit, a white shirt and a tie with stripes and a little badge on it. He is also carrying a brown leather bag, the kind of bag that our doctor brings when he visits our house.

As he walks in to put his bag on the table, I notice something else about him. He limps. One of his legs is shorter than the other, and his shoe has a very thick sole on it – maybe three or four inches thick. But he still limps. If I was a faith healer, I think, I probably would want to see if I could fix my limp. And while I was at it, I would do something about my bald head.

I am thinking about this when he turns to me, 'Now young man, it's a bit of eczema is it? Let's have a look, shall we?'

'Having a look' is a bit more difficult than it sounds. I have just had a bath – my mam insisted I was clean before Mr Armstrong arrived. She has then put on my cream – it is really claggy – it doesn't absorb into my skin; it's a paste that stays there, and on top of that she has bandaged me up. The bandages are to stop the cream from going on to my clothes.

'Show him your arms, pet,' she suggests. 'It's not so serious there.' It's not, and she hasn't bandaged that – just around my knees and my hands. I pull up my sleeve and show him the red patches on the inside of my elbow. He looks at them very carefully, turns to my mam and says, 'Yes, infantile eczema. I see a lot of it.'

And then to me, he says, 'Anthony, is it? Well, Anthony, we will see what the power of prayer can do to make you better.' And he smiles at me. He has the creepiest smile I have ever seen, and I look towards my mam. She is also smiling, but in a comforting way.

He puts his hand on the top of my head and then his whole body becomes very still. I can see his face; I notice that his eyes are closed, and that his lips are moving. He is saying something, but too quietly for me to hear, even though I am right next to him. He is praying.

After a few moments, he stops his praying, takes his hand from my head and looks at me again.

'I have spoken to Him, and he says it will be all right. God will cure you if you have faith in His works.'

His 'works'? What does he mean?

Mam comes to my rescue. 'He's a very good boy, Mr Armstrong. He's in the choir at St George's.'

'Excellent.' replies this very strange man, 'That's a very good start.' I can't help thinking that it hasn't worked very successfully up until now. I've been a choirboy for at least two years, and my eczema seems to be getting worse, not better.

The man is now looking into his leather bag, deciding what he is going to take out. I am worried that he might have some of those doctors' things, and that he is going to start poking me or looking in my ears with that telescope thing with a light. I hope he doesn't do that because I know that my ears are not very clean.

But no, he has found what he is looking for. He has a little brown paper packet in his hands now. It is twisted at the top. He asks my mam for a saucer, and when she brings it, he untwists the packet, and tips the contents of it into the saucer.

Hundreds of tiny white pills.

'Anthony,' he says. 'I want you to take six of these pills, three times every day, after meals.'

'Six pills?' my mam says, 'He's only ten years old. Are they strong?'

'Yes, they are strong,' he says, but not in a medical way. 'They are perfectly safe, but their strength comes from our faith in the Lord. He has made these pills very strong, and if Anthony believes – and you will believe, won't you Anthony?' - again that creepy smile, 'If he truly believes, the power of Our Lord will find its way to curing you, my boy.' He then puts has hand back on my head, stays still and silent for a few seconds and then he grasps me tightly and pulls me towards him.

It's like a cuddle, but it is not a cuddle – it is definitely not a cuddle! I can't wait to get away from him!

He turns towards my mam and starts talking to her about carrot juice. As they are talking, I pick up one of the little pills from the saucer and I pop it into my mouth. It melts – just like icing sugar.

Carrot juice, or as he says, 'the juice of the carrot' is the other medicine that I must take – and I must make it myself, if its healing properties are to work properly. I am to grate some carrots each night and then, using a clean white hankie, I am to squeeze the grated carrot into juice. I must then drink it immediately. I don't know why I just can't eat a carrot, and I don't want to ask this strange man any questions. I want to see him go.

And he does. He insists on shaking my hand, after he has shaken my mam's. He gives me that smile again, tells me how much he is looking forward to seeing me again, and off he limps.

'What did you think of Mr Armstrong?' My mam's first words after closing the door.

'I didn't like him, Mam.'

She looks at me and says, 'Good. Phew!'

'What do you mean?'

'I don't want that man to come within a million miles of our house again. Ughhhh! I hope you don't mind, Anthony, but I think I would rather you had eczema. Sorry, pet. I didn't mean to sound cruel.'

'It's all right, Mam, I know what you mean.'

She laughs. 'I am so pleased,'

I point to the pills on the saucer, 'I think that these are icing sugar, anyway.'

She lights a cigarette and takes a deep drag, blowing out the cigarette smoke before she says, 'That man was the scariest person I have ever met – and I have met some scary people. I'll tell your dad that he's not to come back here – ever!'

'What about the carrot juice, Mam?'

'Do you want to try it?'

95

'I don't mind. Yes, I suppose so.'

'I'll get some carrots when the shops open tomorrow.'

'Do I have to grate them and then use a hankie to …?'

'Of course not. Just eat a carrot every day. Same thing, much easier.'

And I agree. The carrot juice idea is ok if I just eat a carrot. I like carrots. I don't see how it will cure my eczema, but I will give it a try.

My mam says, 'So, Anthony, shall we have lobster for our tea? That sounds very grand, doesn't it?'

'Mmmm,' I say, 'I'm not sure that I like lobster, Mam.'

'Tell you what,' she says. 'I don't want the thing walking around all night. What happens if it escapes from the sink? So, I think we should cook it anyway. I'll also make you some potato fritters, and if you don't like the lobster, you can still have something that you do like. How about that?'

I agree, at least, I say yes. I've just looked at the lobster and I think that he will find some way of attacking me.

'I'll feed Glenda first and put her to bed then we'll have a special lobster dinner together. I am looking forward to that now – you can be my dinner date tonight.' And she puts her arms around me – and yes, that is what a proper cuddle feels like.

Our lobster dinner turns out to be quite successful – if you are happy to accept that we have no lobster. We both eat potato fritters, and to be fair, we both like them, but the lobster …?

We didn't have a pan big enough – that was the first thing. Mam went next door to Auntie Madge's and borrowed a huge pan from her. She filled it with water and then she put it on the stove. She lit two gas rings and eventually the water in the pan began to bubble.

'It's boiling.' she says to me, 'Say goodbye to Mr Lobster.'

My mam is very brave. She reaches into the sink and grabs the lobster, just behind its head. It starts wriggling and tries to use its claws, but they have strong elastic bands around them.

It is too big for the pot. Because it is moving and wriggling, my mam can't just put it into the pot and it slips over the side of the pan and on to the floor. Mam picks it up again, and this time, as she puts it into the pot, she forces it below the boiling water by holding her rolling pin and pressing down on it.

And this is the first reason why we didn't have lobster for our meal. It squealed! It made a noise just like a baby crying. As we watched it, its eyes misted over, and it started to change colour from blue to pink. My mam held it down under the boiling water and it soon stopped moving.

'That's it, I think, Anthony. We'll leave it for a few more minutes and then we'll take it out. I'll get your dad's hammer and pliers. Just keep an eye on it, but don't go near the stove. Shout for me if anything happens.'

'What's going to happen, mam?'

'Well,' my mam says, 'it might want to jump out and chase you.'

'What?'

'Just joking! Back in a minute.'

The longest minute of my life. Nothing happened, the lobster did not rear out of the pan and come seeking me. My mam brought the hammer and pliers that Dad kept in the wash house, and then she switched off the gas.

'We'll let it cool down, Chicken, and then we'll eat it.'

'What's the hammer for, Mam?'

'You've seen how strong the shell is pet, and those claws. The meat is inside the shell, so we have got to break it. The hammer will help us.'

I know they serve lobster in restaurants. 'Do you have to use a hammer when you eat lobster in a restaurant, Mam?'

'I have never eaten lobster in a restaurant, pet, but I suppose, no. The chef will do all that for you – in the kitchen. Just like I am going to do now.' And she smiles at me as she pours the hot water - and the now dead lobster - into the sink.

The second reason that we don't have lobster that day was because my mam has so much difficulty breaking the claws and getting in to the body of the lobster. She hurt her finger too – hitting the lobster claw with too much anger. Eventually, she turns to me and says, 'I'll leave this for your dad. Maybe we can have lobster salad tomorrow? Now, it really was potato fritters that you wanted, wasn't it?'

And it was.

Eleven
The Dad Thing

'To find out if he really loved me, I hooked him up to a lie detector. And just as I suspected, my machine was broken.' Dark Zoo

The most enjoyable part my childhood took place in Hartington Road. This is, I realise, a relative notion, but it was the place where I seemed to be happiest. My life was good; it was a proper childhood, just as it should have been. In addition, because I was the only child in a wider family of very old people, I got a lot of `attention; my mam loved me and so did my grandma.

Yes, my dad and my grandad were a bit gruff, but they were both there, and in their own way, I knew that they cared for me too. Also, on my radar, but as more distant objects, were Uncle John and my great grandma, 'Granny', living in Wallsend Road, not interacting with me when we went around to see them, but just there as a constant.

'As well as those relatives, there were my grandma's sisters: Bess, Belle and Charlotte and their husbands too – Billy, Harry and Tommy. Belle had a daughter, Margaret, but we very rarely saw her. Even within our pretty ordinary family, there was a kind of stratification that seemed to have taken place.

Maybe it was because my mam had married Stan, maybe it was because Belle and Harry were snobs – or because Harry, and therefore the rest of his family – were Catholics. I thought they were snobs: Harry read gas meters for a job, but he was one of the most opinionated men I have ever known. His opening gambit was always, 'As I say ...And he seemed to know everything about everything, and he was always right. Always.

Margaret was about my mam's age, and she became a librarian. She struck lucky, marrying a bright young chap from a university, Cambridge no less, and had a couple of children, both girls.

And that was that. I think that they actively kept a distance from us, as we had virtually nothing to do with them. With these people, as with the members of my extended family, there was always an edginess when anything slightly out of the ordinary occurred, and I am sure that my dad and all he represented, was the reason for this.

Whenever we met any of this extended family of mine - normally at Wallsend Road, they were pleasant enough, not openly hostile, but their attitudes were old, distant – and, something that I picked up on very early – completely devoid of any spark of humour. They never laughed; they never seemed to enjoy anything at all, and their greatest pleasure – and this applied to all of them – seemed to be whenever they could stop me from enjoying myself. They seemed to enjoy saying no to me and stopping me from doing anything at all that might give me any pleasure.

I realised that theirs was a view of the world that needed escaping from. I would need to escape, and I did so eventually, but during these early years, their world view was all that I had to measure anything against. That is what I did, and I found myself seeing everything through a prism that had been constructed out of views that were outdated even before the century had begun.

My closest relatives, at least the relatives with whom I came into contact most frequently, were at least two generations removed from me – and their approach to life had been defined by their various experiences of two world wars - so to me they always seemed so very old in everything they said or did. It was the first world war that created the family relationships in the first place, and the second that sent them into meltdown - when my father arrived in Tynemouth.

My own grandfather, Francis May, was originally from the Gorbals in Glasgow, and had signed up as a drummer boy at the beginning of the first war. He was under age when he signed up and was immediately sent to the Front. He saw action as a Lewis gun operator and was barely seventeen when he was wounded in the leg, invalided out of France and sent to Tynemouth to recuperate – with a war pension for the rest of his life.

It was there that he encountered the Blain girls. The girls were enthusiastic members of the League of Friends, volunteers attached to the Victoria Jubilee Infirmary on Hawkeys Lane, and their duties involved assisting in the rehabilitation of some of the young men who had been wounded in France.

Frank tried, as any young man would, to develop a relationship with the girls, and apparently went down the line until he found one of the sisters who would accept him as a husband. Charlotte, then Bess then Belle all refused him; Jenny accepted.

After they were married, Frank and Jenny seem to have tried very hard to make a respectable domestic life for themselves. Frank got his job for the council as a rent collector, played bowls very well and joined a temperance Masonic lodge. Jenny stayed with the League of Friends, continuing to fundraise for them, and when Agnes, my mam was born, they began to bring her up as a young lady.

Although Mam passed the entrance exam for the grammar school, Frank and Jenny could not afford the fees to send her. They did try other means to broaden her horizons. She learned to play the piano – and I suspect that it was her learning to play the piano that was the cause of her undoing – if meeting and marrying my dad, Stan, was indeed that. This was the law of unintended consequences at work, with a very ironic twist.

Agnes joined the ATS when the war broke out, and then began to train as a nurse. Just like her mother before her in the first war, Agnes looked after injured soldiers in the second – including some who were German. She also met the English lads who were stationed in Tynemouth, one of whom turned out to be Stan.

He played the piano – she played the piano: obviously, a perfect chat up line was there for the making. And even if the chap doing the chatting up was a married man with two children – and in his mid-thirties, Agnes seemed prepared to go against everything that she had ever learned, and everything she had ever been taught, to be with Stan. It had to be the piano that was the cause of all this.

And her name changed. She was 'Agnes' to the family, and 'Mac' to everybody else. She picked up her nickname because of her habit of taking her raincoat (her Mackintosh) with her everywhere she went, and my dad picked up on that and renamed her. Her nickname stayed with her for the rest of her life.

I know I would not be here to offer an opinion of any kind had these events not happened, but however she met him, her meeting the man who became my father was quite simply, a dreadful mistake. It became a tragedy, for her, for my grandparents and ultimately, for me and for my sisters.

It changed my mother from being a cheerful, talented, lively, but somewhat naïve young woman - ready to go out into the world and meet the young man who would bring her happiness - into a thirty-five-year-old widow with four children to look after. And her marriage was probably bigamous.

My own arrival seems to have caused the family some embarrassment too. I have a copy of a marriage certificate that suggests that my mam was probably pregnant when she 'married'. A red official stamp on the certificate says, 'This certificate has been tampered with'.

It was a different world then; these things mattered. 'Out of wedlock', 'bastard', these are terms that would have huge resonance at that time, and I can only imagine what they meant to my mam's strait-laced family.

They were not built to take that kind of strain – neither was my mam, poor lass. No wonder there was a bit of tension in the air when Stan and my mam had to move into Wallsend Road. And I became the living symbol of everything that had gone wrong with Agnes' life.

Add to that this: in researching for this book, I typed my father's name into Google and out came a version of his life. I saw his date of birth, his parents, Adele, his Belgian wife, his children (his other children, Pamela and Marie) and the place and cause of his death.

However, something was missing – any mention of us, the family that he had created on Tyneside. Everything that had happened to him had happened south of London. There is no mention of Tynemouth, of his marriage to my mother, and by extension, no mention of me or of my sisters.

As far as Mr Google is concerned, we have never existed. His life seems to have been lived in and around Carshalton in Surrey. Well, Mr Google, I and my five children, along with my three sisters and their assorted offspring, would like you to know that not only do we exist, we have clawed ourselves out of the pit that our errant father left us in.

I've told you that my dad was a musician, a pianist, and apparently quite a good one too. A pre-war identity card of his lists 'musician' as his occupation. He told me that he had played with Max Jaffa, quite a big star in those days, and that he had also played in a summer season at Blackpool, where he was known as 'The Poor Man's Rex Harrison'.

Long after, when I was a young man myself, my mam confirmed all this. She added that he had been friends with Joan Rhodes, a very famous 'strong woman' who toured variety theatres for years and years, tearing up telephone directories and bending six-inch nails.

She also mentioned that Frankie Howerd, now a very famous comedian, had also visited us on several occasions. I have no evidence to support either of these claims, but as she had no reason to lie, I am happy to believe her.

Stan was a self-taught pianist; unable to read music, but able to pick up any melody immediately. He'd played in various dance bands before and during the war. I also know that he left school at thirteen to become apprenticed to an organ maker. When he lived with us he played the piano in various working men's clubs on a regular basis – at least three or four nights a week. And often at weekends too.

Another area where I suppose I must have disappointed him, is that even with two parents who both played the piano, I showed no musical ability at all. If I could have been a young Mozart, things might have been different, but as I had a 'tin ear' as he would say, yet another possible bonding opportunity was lost on us.

I've since learned to play the guitar passably well, and being a Geordie at heart, I have even tried to get a tune out of the Northumbrian pipes; three of my own kids are good musicians as we had them taught properly. The opportunity was there for me to learn: we may have been poor, but we had a Bechstein upright piano in the house, and that was just another of the many squandered opportunities that defined the early part of my life.

My dad, Stan, was tall, and 'saturnine' is maybe the word that best describes him – a sallow complexion, high cheekbones, world-weary look – totally and absolutely the wrong kind of person to end up with my mother. He was six foot one; she was five foot nothing, apart from anything else. And his subsequent behaviours including a host of affairs, defined the relationship that developed between him and his innocent and naïve second wife.

Things eventually came to a head when he fell for a young blonde bus conductor whom he frequently saw as, two or three evenings a week, he took the Hunter's bus to a working men's club at Seaton Delaval where he played the piano. This relationship produced yet another child, a boy, and a wish from him that he move on, separate from us, his second family, and set up, for a third time, with his new woman, the twenty-one-year-old Mary.

We're pushing ahead a little, as all this happened some six or so years after we moved to Hartington Road. But as it effectively ended my childhood, it helps to explain why those five or six years in our first new house were so important to me.

One afternoon, we were in our second new council house, this time in Stanton Road. I was ten, Glenda was six, my second sister Marion was a tiny baby, and my mam had just become pregnant with Patricia.

On this afternoon, and completely by surprise, Dad and his new woman, Mary, came to the house. Mam immediately sent me and Glenda upstairs, but we sat at the top of the stairs and listened while my father told our mother that he wanted a separation from her - and us, and that he was going to move out of our house and set up with Mary in Seaton Delaval.

I think that my mother was more offended than anything else by their daring to come to our house and violating her space – our space. She was very upset and became hysterical at one point - I don't know how much of this scenario she was already aware of, but she was crying so much that I know I decided that she needed some help, and I went downstairs to intervene.

I am not sure what I had intended to do, but before I could do anything, my father lashed out at me, catching me with an open-handed slap around the head. This hurt, and in a moment, he had turned me around, shouted that I go back upstairs and given me a sharp push.

Glenda was at the top of the stairs, and she held my hand while we both quietly wept. That was the closest, most intimate moment I ever had with my sister Glenda. From then on, things changed so much and so quickly that any chance of normal sibling relationships was ended forever.

And one more event from this period overshadows everything that has ever happened in my life even to this day. And it is the pathos of the set of circumstances, the simple sadness of it all, not the hurt, not the anger, that has me push the same thoughts around in my mind time after time, and always without any sense of resolution.

We had been living at Stanton Road for a couple of years or so. My sister Marion had been born; I got to choose the name of my new sister and she was called after Marion Thompson, John Thompson's sister – somebody a little older than me and with whom I was hopelessly in love.

Also, eleven months after Marion's arrival, my third sister, Patricia, came along. She was a real surprise – right in the middle of the 'Mary' fiasco, my dad had managed to father yet another child.

So, now with four children by my mother, one baby in Seaton Delaval and God knows what compromises having been arrived at, my father, who had apparently not left us for Mary but continued to live at home, chose to return, for whatever reason, to visit what had been his first family in Carshalton in Surrey.

There he stayed with his former wife (Adele, a Belgian woman who carried a torch for him long after he had died) and their two young daughters, Marie and Pamela. He had gone to London ostensibly because of his work at the Ministry of Pensions, having recently been promoted to Executive Officer (EO), and at the time we did not even know that he was staying with his former wife and the girls.

One night, he went to bed (he was sleeping downstairs on the settee, I believe), carefully sealed the door of the living room with newspapers, turned on the gas - and killed himself. He was forty-seven years old – coincidentally, the same age as my mam was when she died.

With both of my parents dead at forty-seven, you will realise how relieved I was when I reached my forty-eighth birthday.

What a guy! And do you know what is the truly weird thing about me and my dad? Despite what he did, I still think about him almost every day.

Oh – a sad postscript. I don't know what happened to Mary – or to her son, my half-brother? I did see Mary some years later when I was a passenger on a Hunter's bus, just like my dad had been. I had turned into a yob by then, I was probably drunk - that was a normal state for me – and I was with my mates, and I said deeply offensive things to her, on that bus, that I have always regretted saying.

I can't remember exactly what I did say - the actual words themselves, but I know that I saw that girl, and she was just a girl, wrongly. I saw her as evil, as the person who had destroyed our family. She wasn't evil, of course: she was simply another victim – just like the rest of us. Poor lass, I hope she managed to salvage something of a life. I did, most of us did. I really hope that she did too.

Twelve
A Tale of Two Cinemas
Cinema One – The Regal, West Monkseaton

'If I had known then, what I still don't know now.' John Betjeman

Every Saturday my mam gives me some money for my bus fare. I take the number 12 from the stop across the road near where the new fire station is being built, and I get off at the bus station in Whitley Bay. I then take a second bus from Whitley Bay up to Dale Road in West Monkseaton where my Auntie Charlotte lives. On my way home, after I have had my tea, I do the same thing but the other way around.

At least, that is what I am supposed to do. I've being going to see Auntie Charlotte for maybe ten times now, always on Saturdays. But now, unless it is raining, I get off the bus in Whitley Bay and, instead of catching the next bus as I am supposed to, I walk up Marine Drive and Cauldwell Lane to my Auntie's

I do the same thing when I am going home, so I can save my bus fare down to Whitley Bay too. That means that every Saturday night I have some money in my pocket to spend, and a short time where my auntie thinks I am going home, and my mam and dad also think the same thing.

But I'm not: I am in The Spanish City! I have money – not very much, but enough to play the games that I enjoy the most. I prefer the amusement arcade where I can have a go on my favourite pinball machines, but sometimes, if my auntie gives me a couple of bob for pocket money, and if I already have my bus fares saved, I go straight into the Spanish City itself to spend my money on the pinball machines and my current favourite, the racing cars – not the dodgems, although I like them, but the cars that you can race around a circuit.

Once a few weeks ago, just after I arrived at Dale Road, I found a pound note on the floor by the kitchen table. I picked it up and put it in my pocket. I was waiting all day for my auntie to ask me about it, but she said nothing at all. That evening, before I caught the bus back home, I had ten goes on the racing cars, one after the other.

The Spanish City has been in right at the centre of my imagination since I was about three years old. I had never been there until recently, but lots and lots of people who are lucky enough to go there – mostly kids I play with - came into school on a Monday morning saying how magical the place was; how it is like all your wishes coming true at the same time.

And it is. They are right! My all-time favourite dream is my dream of driving a car, and at the Spanish City I can do that. My other dreams: shooting a real gun with real bullets, winning prizes from a machine with a big crane that has a claw on the end of it, getting a giant candy floss and keeping it all to myself – these dreams are all there, and they all come true.

This place is like a dream - it is full of people laughing; enjoying huge cones of pink candyfloss - and ice cream that's in a dozen different colours and flavours - not the vanilla flavour white stuff that we sometimes have as a treat at home – and they all have chocolate flakes in them – and everybody is laughing and joking as they move from ride to ride, from machine to machine – and that, I think, it what I like the best. People laughing, being happy and making jokes: I do miss that at home – and my Auntie Charlotte and my Uncle Tom don't even smile, never mind laugh.

The Spanish City in Whitley Bay can be seen from miles away: it has a huge, shiny white dome that you can see in the daytime, especially if the sun is shining, and it's all lit up at night, so you just can't miss it.

Inside – and it's free to get in - there are roundabouts, shooting galleries, stalls of all kinds – and the machine arcades, of course. There are hundreds of different slot machines: machines where you can win prizes, machines where you can play games, and a special game that I like almost as much as I like the pinball machines and the racing cars.

This, my third favourite machine, is called 'Rear Gunner'. You have a machine gun, with a red button – from a real plane - to fire and everything. You look through the eyepiece and you see the German planes coming towards you – or flying away from you. Then you fire the gun at them, and sometimes they explode.

I am not sure if the planes explode because I have fired the gun at them. The film of the planes flying at you is very old and grainy, but I get very excited with 'Rear Gunner', and sometimes I prefer to spend all my money on that machine, and not on the racing cars or even the pinball machines with the flippers, even though I like those most of all.

I thought that I might go on 'Rear Gunner' tonight on my way home; I will have enough money for two or three goes if I save my bus fare, but my Auntie Charlotte says she has a treat for me today. She tells me that at the Regal, the cinema just across the road from her house, there is a film on this afternoon that she knows I will love.

She knows that I like cowboys – my Uncle Tom used to bring me Roy Rogers toys when he came home from sea - and because 'The Man from Laramie' is on at the Regal, she says that she will pay for me to go and will also give me sixpence to buy a drink or some popcorn.

I am so excited! I have wanted to see 'The Man from Laramie' for ages: I already know most of the words to the song, and if only I had known, I would have brought one of my cowboy guns with me today.

This is quite unusual for Auntie Charlotte, because she doesn't like spending money. I don't think that she even likes me coming on a Saturday, but she says she does it to give my mam a rest. Marion, my new sister is crying a lot at home, and Mam has a new baby, Patricia, to look after now. And, of course, my dad is no longer around. He died when he was away in London. My mam is very tired, and she cries a lot too.

Auntie Charlotte lives with Uncle Tom in Dale Road. Uncle Tom used to be a sailor, but he became ill in somewhere called the 'Persian Gulf' and had to stop being a sailor. He is quite a clever man, I think, because he was a chief engineer on his ship, but now he works as a draughtsman at Swan Hunters. My Uncle John has also worked there, not as a draughtsman, he was a fitter, but he doesn't work there now.

The strange thing is this: Auntie Charlotte and Uncle Tom don't seem to like each other very much. When I am at their house, they don't like being in the same room together. They have been married for years and years, but Uncle Tom was always at sea. Now he lives at home all the time and when they are in the same room together, they always seem to be quarrelling.

Last week, Uncle Tom told me that Auntie Charlotte 'wouldn't let me have children'. I didn't know you needed permission, and I didn't know how to answer. But Uncle Tom is sad. He told me he always wanted children, but it is too late now.

Maybe that is why he always brought me presents back from when he was at sea? I don't get those presents from him now because he doesn't go to sea any more – and yesterday, he 'retired' from his job at Swans.

That means he won't be going back to work there on Monday – or ever again, he tells me. They have already cancelled the papers, and that, I don't understand at all.

I like the Regal cinema. I have been here two times before. The manager is a funny looking little man with a hunchback, and he is always angry. He walks up and down the aisle shining his torch at people while the film is on, and he keeps on asking them to stop doing things.

'The Man from Laramie' is the film I have come to see, but it is not on yet. I have come to see a cowboy film in colour, but the Movietone News is on now, and it is in black and white and the man is talking about boring things. I have just bought my popcorn from the kiosk and I am going back to my seat.

I hear the voice of a girl, and she is talking to me: 'My friend says she would like you to sit next to her.' I look at where the voice is coming from and I see a young girl, very pretty and about my age. She is smiling. 'Do you want to sit next to her?' she whispers.

The manager is coming down the aisle towards us, shining his torch. There are not many people in the cinema, so I think he is coming to talk to us. The girl points and I see her friend; she is also smiling. I move towards her and sit down next to her before the manager reaches us, and he walks down to the front of the rows and goes out of a door at the bottom which is hidden by a curtain.

'What's your name?' the girl says.

'Anthon.... – Tony. My name is Tony,' I reply. I am very pleased that the cinema is dark because I am sure that I am blushing, and my hands are picking away at the top of my packet of Butterkist.

'I'm Suzanne', she says to me, 'and this is Jeannie' pointing to her friend who is now sitting at the other side of her.

I don't know what to say – I have no words. A girl. I've never talked to a strange girl like this before. The girls at school never show much interest in me. They are not nasty to me, but my arms and legs are dry and wrinkly with eczema. I put cream from the doctor on it every night, but it doesn't go away. In the dark, the eczema doesn't show.

'Where do you live?' Suzanne whispers to me, and I can feel her breath on my ears. 'North Shields - Marden', I manage to stutter in reply. I am whispering too, and although I am very close to her, I don't dare to look at her eyes. But our heads are very close to each other.

'How old are you, Tony?' is her next question, and I wonder if I should lie. I am only eleven – should I say I am twelve, or thirteen?

'Twelve – I am nearly twelve. H – How old are you?' 'I'm eleven', she replies, 'and Jeannie will be eleven next month.'

'What school do you go to?' I tell her that I am at Monkhouse Junior school on the Marden Estate. She does not know it; she goes to school in Monkseaton – and she is in the same class as Jeannie.

'Why are you here at the Regal, then?' That is an easier question to answer, and I am able to explain how I come to visit my auntie in Dale Road every week, and how she knows I wanted to see this film.

'What number in Dale Road?'

At that moment, my film comes on, 'The Man from Laramie', and I pretend to be interested in it. My head is spinning, and I want to talk to this girl, but I have no idea what to say. I open my Butterkist and offer her some. Jeannie also takes some, and I try to concentrate on the song because I know the words and I have been waiting to hear Frankie Laine singing it for so long. But it doesn't matter anymore. This girl beside me is all that matters.

And she asks again, 'What number in Dale Road?'

'Number eight,' I stumble with my reply, and spill some of my Butterkist on to the floor and on to her skirt. 'Sorry. I didn't ...'

'It's all right, it doesn't matter,' and she brushes the Butterkist from her skirt. 'I live in Mitchell Avenue. I walk past that house every day.'

Frankie Laine is singing the song now. I want to listen to how he makes the words sound - and the film has started.

We say nothing – but I feel that I am on fire. My heart is beating so loudly that I am sure that everyone else in the cinema can hear it too. I hear Suzanne breathing, and then she turns to Jeannie and says something that I can't hear. Jeannie giggles and whispers back.

Suzanne turns to me, and for the first time, I look at her. We are in the dark, but in the light of the film, where I see James Stewart riding on his horse, and, as well as the 'Winchester 73' rifle that he has in a holster on his saddle, he is carrying the same kind of revolver that my Uncle Tom bought for me all those years ago – except that mine was golden: his is not.

Suzanne is holding my hand. A minute ago, our hands touched as I was removing a piece of Butterkist from my trouser leg, and she took a hold of my hand. My right hand and her left hand. Do I move? Do I turn to look at her? I don't know what to do.

Sometimes my eczema affects not just my legs and arms, but my hands, and then I often have keens on my knuckles. If I touch a dog – or any animal, I get a rash, but sometimes it is more serious. When that happens, I must have cream and bandages on my hands, but I am so pleased that, just now my hands are clear - and I can enjoy the touch of this girl – a girl I have only just met – holding my hand – my hand.

Suzanne has my hand in both of hers now. We do not look at each other. My hand is in her lap, and she lifts it and places it palm down on to her thigh. I can feel her thigh – and I also feel a sort of button thing as well. My mam has those – she calls them 'suspenders'.

I don't know what to do, I don't know what to think. Am I supposed to...? We have not talked for maybe five or even ten minutes. We are both watching the film while pretending to be unaware of what is really happening. I am only eleven; I have a rough idea of what might happen – I do have two sisters, and I am aware of how different they look from me. I am also aware of my own body, and how I am feeling very excited while Suzanne moves my hand up and down her thigh so very slowly.

She breaks our silence. She holds my hand a little more tightly, moves her mouth close to my ear, and whispers so that only I can hear: 'You can do anything you want to me.'

I bloom – I am sure that my head is going to explode, but what she says to me does not help. What does she mean? We are sitting side by side in a cinema, after all. Her friend, Jeannie is sitting next to her. There are not very many people in the cinema, but there are quite a few of them near to us. There are certain things we can't do, obviously, but what can we do? And isn't this so wrong? Will I get into trouble whatever I do?

The problem is solved in an immediate and quite unpleasant manner. A torch shines on to us. The manager has come down the aisle, and neither of us notices. He sees me holding Suzanne's hand, and barks out – so that everyone can hear: 'What do you think you are doing? Hey, come here you. How old are you – fiddling around with that young girl? She's a child; she's a bloody child.'

'I'm eleven – twelve.' I stutter.

'You'll go to prison for this, lad. Come on – out of there.' I stand up – I don't want to go, but a grown up is telling me to do something, and that talk about prison has got me very worried. What will my mam say if I have to go to prison? Worse, what will my dad say?

Just as I get up to go, Suzanne looks up at me and says, 'See you next week?' I mutter a response, but my embarrassment at being taken to the door of the cinema by the manager – by this strange looking little man with a big hump on his shoulder, a man who is much shorter than I am, but because he is the manager is making me feel stupid and embarrassed.

And his torch is shining directly into my eyes. I can't answer, and I stumble to the exit and out of the front door and into the bright light of the afternoon. In doing so, I leave Suzanne and Jeannie, and James

Stewart and Frankie Laine and do you know what – I have no wish to see 'The Man from Laramie' again.

I am at Auntie Charlotte's now – hoping that the cinema manager has not followed me. I am explaining to my auntie how the film snapped, and the manager told everybody that they had to leave the cinema because they couldn't fix the film. My uncle Tom is suspicious, I can tell. I hope he doesn't go over the Regal and check up on my story because even I know that it is not a very good one.

Then I have an idea. I ask my uncle Tom if I can listen to my new record on his radiogram. He is very proud of his radiogram and it can play six records at a time. We go into his music room and the radiogram is right next to his piano. Uncle Tom recently had a seven-foot extension built to his music room so that he could keep his piano there. It is a baby grand, and my dad says that it is a 'fine instrument'.

My new record is 'Diana' by Paul Anka, and I bought it last week with some money my grandma gave me. I brought it to Aunt Charlotte's because we don't have a record player at home, and I played it about fifty times – so Uncle Tom said. I will keep it in Dale Road and add it to the small collection of records that Uncle Tom allows me to play. They include an EP of 'My Fair Lady' and a record by Noel Coward, 'Mad Dogs and Englishmen', and on the other side, 'Don't put your daughter on the stage, Mrs Worthington'.

I am hoping today that if I can play my songs on the radiogram, it will take my uncle Tom's mind off thinking about the lie I have told. I don't like lying, but I couldn't think of anything else to say, and I am still worried that the cinema manager might find out where I am.

I was going to go to the Spanish City on my way home this afternoon: I think that it would be better if I don't.

I am looking forward to next Saturday already. I think I am in love, and I can't wait to see Suzanne again.

Thirteen
A Tale of Two Cinemas
Cinema Two – The Picture House, Whitley Bay
'I wish I didn't know now what I didn't know then' Bob Seger

My attitude towards the cinema has always been ambivalent: note I am not talking about the 'movie theatre' and 'movies', in fact, not even about the 'cinema', but about the 'pictures' and 'films', pronounced 'filums', thank you! And I quite often continue to pronounce the word that way nowadays - it seems to get up the nose of people, but that's the correct pronunciation of my childhood– filums!

I love the cinema, but it worries me too: more specifically, I am troubled by what has always been my fascination with it – and in retrospect, I worry that I could have been held so much in its thrall for so long.

For years, my cinema going was a truly secret vice, a vice which started at about the age of ten. I discovered its capacity to excite – beyond any action that might have been happening on the screen, and much of my adolescence and youth was spent in finding ways both to see films that I ought not to have been seeing, and spending time with people whom I ought to have been avoiding.

I didn't go very often, and hardly at all with my family. My dad had once taken me to see 'The Dam Busters' when it came out, and I could understand why he wanted to see that film. It was patriotic, and he had been in the army for six years.

But 'Annie Get Your Gun'? Why he wanted to see that film was a complete mystery to me. It involved two bus journeys preceded by a long walk to the bus stop.

The reason that the film was of so much interest to him became a little more obvious when we chose our seats in the cinema. He immediately sat next to a young woman who said hello to me and smiled. I was embarrassed as I said hello to her, but the film had just started, and our conversation ended.

I was too young to understand what was going on, but I had a rough idea that this was something that my dad was keeping secret from my mam.

When you become party to a secret, what do you do? Especially when this secret involves it being kept from your mam? Well, in my case, I simply lost interest in going to the pictures with my dad. He picked up on this; he didn't push it, but I think he knew why, and he only suggested it once or twice after that.

I think that I always managed to find some excuse, or something else to do. For whatever reason, he wasn't particularly interested in pursuing the matter, and picture-going with my dad ground to something of a desultory halt.

That didn't stop me from wanting to go to the pictures, but I wanted to be able to go by myself. It was my greatest ambition to be able to get in to see a film at the Picture House in Whitley Bay. That was where they showed the kind of films that every eleven-year-old boy wanted to see but couldn't. These 'A' and 'X' rated pictures were the holy grail of my adolescence. These were pictures that we could proudly talk about to our friends if we had managed to get in – one way or another.

The 'X' rated films were impossible for me, as you had to be sixteen, but if I could pass for twelve, I could see an 'A' film. That would have meant that my parents would have had to accompany me, but the kind of 'A' picture that I was hoping to see was not one that I would wish to see with my parents.

By now there were certain kinds of 'adult' films that were of particular interest to me. I hadn't seen any of them yet, but I knew what I wanted to see. We're talking breasts here, that's all – that's the then limit of my ambition. My imagination wasn't of the order of a modern-day teenager, aged and jaded beyond belief by the torrents of porn that are universally available now. No, I simply wanted to see a breast – or more specifically, a nipple.

I had seen a nipple before, obviously, but that particular nipple belonged to my mother, and with the best will in the world, I couldn't warm to that thought – and it still disturbs me.

The Picture House in Whitley Bay was the place to go to see 'that kind of film', the sort of adult picture that I was longing for, one which might offer the occasional glimpse of partial nudity – and that was all I craved. My tastes were simple enough, but they did obsess me.

My plan was to choose my time carefully, and then I was going to hang around the entrance of the Picture House and encourage an adult to take me in – I could only see an 'A' film if I was accompanied by an adult.

It seemed a good plan to me. I had to pass through Whitley Bay on my way to West Monkseaton, so it was conveniently on my way, I could find the time to watch a film by making an excuse for either my mam or Auntie Charlotte. Any local newspaper would tell me what was on, and also whether either of the pictures that would be showing that day was an 'A' and was going to be worth my while taking the risk.

Of course, it wasn't just what was happening on the screen that had excited me. My hopes of that kind were well defined in my own mind; I knew what I was looking to see, but since I had started going to West Monkseaton to see my Auntie Charlotte, my Saturday afternoon visits to the Regal had suddenly kindled my cinematic interests in an altogether different way.

I had a new fascination with the cinema: not as an art form, you understand, that was to come later, but not yet. No, my new interest in cinema was more to do with the fascinating darkness of the place, and the secretive, fumbling excitement of being in that very darkness, wondering what the other kids at the matinee were thinking – and if those kids were girls, were they thinking the same things that I was thinking?

I was now developing a strong interest in girls, in females. I did have three sisters by now: Glenda was about seven, Marion was a toddler and Patricia was still gurgling in her pram. They just got in my way – if ever they appeared on my radar – which frankly, they didn't. They were just 'girls'. And I sometimes played out with girls up and down the street, but only when there weren't any boys to play with. When a boy, any boy, turned up, I would happily dump the girls, and any game we were playing.

But suddenly, and it was very suddenly, everything had changed. My sitting next to a girl called Suzanne one Saturday afternoon in the Regal cinema, West Monkseaton, had completely reordered my priorities. Out of the window went my disdain for anything female: to be replaced by – obsession!

Now my only priority – literally, my only thought for one whole week – was to recreate the situation of last weekend when I had sat next to Suzanne in the darkness of the Regal cinema, and she had placed my hand on her thigh. In that moment, I had begun to see the point of leaving childhood behind.

***

The week of waiting before I can get back to Monkseaton seems to have so many more days in it somehow, and each hour of waiting stretches out to be well over sixty minutes. But Saturday does arrive eventually, and I feel so elated, so sharp and vital that I could almost fly there.

More prosaically, I catch the number twelve bus down to Whitley Bay, and to get to West Monkseaton more quickly, I even sacrifice the money that I normally would save, and instead of walking the second part of the journey, I get straight on to the connection at the bus station and pay the fare.

I want to be there, outside the Regal cinema at the very moment the doors open, so that I can look for Suzanne and sit right next to her.

First, however, there is the Auntie Charlotte ritual to go through. On my arrival, there will be a salad - because it is summer. There will be a leaf of lettuce, half a tomato, half a hard-boiled egg, one spring onion, a bottle of Heinz Salad Cream, a slice of white bread, buttered, and a glass of milk. I must get through this first before I can then suggest that I find out what's on at the Regal and can I please go to see the matinee.

I've just arrived at Dale Road and rung the bell. Something is different. There is an atmosphere. Both my aunt and my Uncle Tom have come to the door – that is unusual as normally they avoid each other.

'Did your mother not get my letter, Anthony?' My auntie is the first to speak.

'What letter? Er...no, we didn't get a letter.'

She turns to my uncle. 'Tom, I put that letter in the post-box on Wednesday morning first thing – straight after that girl...'

That girl! My mind is racing. What's been going on? They both look angry, and Uncle Tom looks at me, then up and down the street, and says, 'You'd better come in for a minute, we're not doing this on the step.'

They take me into the front room. We never go in there. I normally listen to my records on Uncle Tom's new radiogram in his music room at the back of the house. It's a summer's day, but the front room is freezing. No salad either. My brief encounter with the salad usually happens in the kitchen, but no – straight into the front room – the room nearest the front door.

They motion me to sit down and then they sit opposite me - together. They never sit down together: this is serious. What have I done? That girl - could it be...?

Uncle Tom starts, 'We had a visit on Tuesday night. It was a bit of a surprise. Your 'girlfriend' came to say hello.' He manages to put an emphasis on the word 'girlfriend' that is more than distasteful: he is disgusted.

'My girlfriend? I don't have a girlfriend, Uncle Tom.' He's talking about Suzanne, that girl I sat next to last week – and who I am hoping to see this afternoon.

Auntie Charlotte butts in, 'It's no use lying to us, Anthony. She told us she that is your girlfriend. That is the word she used – 'girlfriend'. She said her name was Suzanne and she lives in Mitchell Avenue.'

It is her: she said she knew the house where I came every Saturday. I try to defend myself, 'I only met her last week. I said hello to her, that's all. She's not my girlfriend. I don't have a girlfriend.'

Auntie Charlotte continues; she hasn't been listening, 'I wrote a letter to your mother. I told them that we don't approve of that sort of thing, you are far too young to be having a girlfriend, and we said that you weren't to come back here again.'

'We don't want you coming here again,' Uncle Tom says, although I think that I have already got that message.

'But I like coming here!' It's feeble, I know, but my mind is in a whirl. What has been happening? What did Suzanne say? I try again, 'I only spoke to her and her friend at the pictures last week. That was the first time I saw her...'

'I am not interested in your excuses!' Uncle Tom motors on, 'Strange people turning up on our doorstep. This is not what we expected – not what we expected at all! You are going straight back home. I am going take you to the bus stop now, and I will wait with you and make sure that you get on the bus. You are not to come back here next Saturday – or any other Saturday!'

'We are not used to this kind of behaviour,' Auntie Charlotte adds, 'We thought we could help your mother, give her a little break, but this kind of trouble is not what we bargained for. She'll have to make some other arrangements for a Saturday. We don't want to see you again.'

There was nothing I could do, and even less that I could say. Their ludicrous overreaction was typical of all my family. It was mostly because they were old but also because they had never been parents themselves, and their idealistic view of childhood was straight from the nineteenth century. Little boys didn't behave in the way they evidently thought I had been behaving.

After all, a single visit to their doorstep by a young girl doesn't necessarily presage disaster, but this is what they had concluded. It was bizarre, and, truth be told, I was a little young – and so was Suzanne! Part of me could understand why they might be adopting this approach to me now.

But there is no room for such a thought in my mind now. Suzanne! What about her? I want to get to the Regal so that I can sit next to Suzanne. I want to have her take my hand and put it gently on her thigh. I want to feel ...

The brief reverie is interrupted: 'Come on Anthony, up you get. I'll walk you to the bus stop. I want to make sure that you get on that bus.'

And he does. He walks me round to the bus stop in Cauldwell Lane where we wait in embarrassed silence until the bus arrives. I keep looking up towards the corner where the Regal is in the hope that I might catch a glimpse of Suzanne, but I don't see her.

When the bus eventually does arrive, my Uncle Tom watches me get on, and then he tells the bus conductor to make sure that I stay on it until they arrive at the bus station in Whitley Bay. He then asks me if I have the bus fare in my pocket. I have and say so – I am too slow to suggest otherwise - and I sit down on the bench seat at the back, next to where the conductor normally stands.

The conductor says I am to stay there where he can see me, and by the time I've bought a ticket from him, I've only enough money left to get back to the Marden on the number twelve. Any thoughts of my sneaking back to Monkseaton in the hope of seeing Suzanne are completely goosed. My first ever romance, doomed before it has even begun.

So, it's about half past one in the afternoon and I'm sitting on the bus and on my way home. I am fuming: I'm angry with my auntie and my uncle, I am angry with Suzanne – somebody whom I don't even know. – and I am furious with myself because I know that I could have played this all so differently.

I don't know how, but there must be a better conclusion to this set of events. It's just that I am too stupid to be able to work it out.

As the bus turns off Marine Avenue, just by the Essoldo, it slows down. It's going to stop outside the Spanish City, and the conductor, who has been keeping an eye on me is upstairs now. I decide that before he is there to prevent me, I will make my escape.

I quickly move to the platform, hold on to the safety rail and then leap off the bus and on to the pavement that leads, not to the Spanish City, but down to the ice cream shops and more importantly, to the arcade and the machines.

Second only to my developing love for the pictures, is my love for the arcades and the slot machines that can be found there. I like the games of skill much more than the gambling games, so I always have a finite amount of money to spend as I don't gamble and can't win any more.

The pinball machines with the flippers that allow you to keep the ball in play are now my real favourites but today, although I am now down in Whitley Bay with hours to kill and pinball machines of every possible kind surrounding me, I have no money. I have enough to get the bus home, but only from the bus station, further up the road.

I wander through the main arcade, up and down the rows of machines, shaking and checking the pay-out trays as I walk by. I am hoping that someone has failed to take all his winnings, or that a rejected coin has not been picked out of the tray, but no luck, the trays are all empty.

As I've got no money for the machines, I'm thinking about maybe going in to the Spanish City to have a look at the rides when a voice says,

'Do you want to play the machines, son?'

It's a man – I don't know him, but he is smiling, and he has a coin that he gives to me. 'Go on, lad. Have a go – this one looks great. Have you played it before?'

Have I played it before? It's my favourite! It's the biggest pinball machine in the arcade and it has hundreds of lights and springs and traps – also double flippers on each side. It's a very popular machine, and usually there are people waiting their turn to play it. But not this afternoon. I take the coin that the man has held out for me, thank him, and I put it into the machine. It lights up, and off I go.

The man is watching me, and he sees each of my first five plays eventually come to an end. My score is not very high – I have done much better before, but maybe because he is watching me, I am not as sharp as usual.

'Try again – you've got a good eye,' he says, and gives me another coin. I try again, and my score this time is almost two thousand better – not my record, but much better than before.

'Do you want another go?' Another coin is offered. I want to play, but I am not comfortable about being given all this money.

'No, it's all right,' I say. 'I've got to go now.'

'Tell you what, we'll play one more game. How about that?'

I really want to play another game – I know I can beat my record.

'I'll play with you,' he says. 'Double flippers – two for you and two for me.'

He puts the coin in the slot. There are two flippers on either side of the machine. I can work one pair of them, and if he stands behind me, he can work the other. This he does, and he is now standing behind me, his arms enclosing me as we play the game.

His breath smells of beer, and I am starting to feel uncomfortable. I enjoy playing this game – and today I have had more goes on it than ever before – but I've never played it with a man standing behind me.

'What's your name, son?' He continues to flip the ball, keeping it in play.

'To – Toby,' why the heck did I give such a stupid name?

'Toby? And where are you from, Toby? Where do you live?'

I'm not going to tell him. I say that I am from Wallsend, and that I am here with my mam and dad for the day.

'My dad will be coming for me soon', I lie, 'Thanks for the game. I have to go now.'

'I'm Walter. Toby, do you like going to the pictures?' He continues to play as he asks me. His arms are still circling me.

'What do you mean?'

'Do you like going to see films?' He pronounces the word like I do, as he continues to flip the ball back into play. 'I bet you do. I'm going round to the Picture House now. Do you want to come with me?'

'I can't. I'm meeting my dad soon,' I continue to make my excuses. But the Picture House. He's going to the Picture House, and 'High School Confidential.' is on this week. I've seen photos of one of the stars of that picture, Mamie van Doren, and she is blonde, beautiful – and that name – I love her name. She's exactly the kind of woman I want to see on the screen!

'Maybe you can come for an hour, and then you can go and meet your dad? It's still early. It's a canny film, you'll like it. That young lass – the blonde one, she does a turn, you knaa.'

And she does a turn! I pretend to understand. I am not sure what he means, but I am very interested. Yes, I tell myself, by rights I should be at the Regal now, sitting next to Suzanne – someone I will never see again if I am not allowed to go back to Monkseaton. And yes, it is only just after two o'clock now, and I don't normally go home on a Saturday until after five.

I, and this man Walter, slowly make our way out of the arcade and down towards the Picture House. The cinema, as I now know, was incorporated into the main building of the Spanish City – originally it was an aquarium, but that didn't work out – and its entrance is in a parade of shops on the Promenade, overlooking The Pleasure Gardens and the sea.

I have been here before, of course: I have walked past the entrance to this place many times, seeing the posters advertising the very films that I so desperately wanted to see.

And yes, on one truly special – and different - occasion a few years ago, I was here when my whole school had lined up, with all the other schools in the area, so that we could watch the new, young Queen Elizabeth drive by, and I stood where I am standing now as her car passed, and in two seconds it was over. I did see her though.

Now, I am about to see my first 'A' film – with Mamie van Doren who, this Walter has assured me – will be doing a turn! I hope that means what I think it is going to mean, but I don't ask him.

I am not comfortable with this whole situation now. I know I might be getting in to the Picture House, but I am weighing that up against the sense of uneasiness that threatens to overwhelm the adventure, and even the risk that I want to take.

The man is odd – his face is flushed, and as we walk down towards the Picture House, he is staying near me, but away from me at the same time. This is wrong, and I know it is wrong.

'Right, Toby. If the lass at the kiosk asks, I'm your dad, ok?'

My dad? I know that I have prepared for this. A theoretical dad. My original plan was for me to ask an adult to allow me to go in with them, but this man, my dad? I look more closely at him. He is not very clean, and his suit has marks on it, grease or food, maybe both. His hand, the one he holds his cigarette in, has yellowish-brown stains on it, much darker than the ones that used to be on my dad's hand. He must smoke a lot of cigarettes.

Walter puts his hand on my shoulder as we turn to climb the few stairs towards the entrance.

I stop as we get to the top of the stairs, and turn to him, 'I better go – my mam and dad will be wondering where I am.'

Walter looks around; he is embarrassed, his eyes looking everywhere, 'It's ok, son,' he is very nervous, 'we'll just go in for a few minutes. If you don't like the film, we'll come out straight away. There's plenty of time. Come on, it's about to start.''

He can see that I am unhappy. I have stopped on the steps and moved away from him. I am not going in. I want to see the film, but not with this man.

'Is that you, Tweddle?' A loud voice comes from behind us. 'Are you with that boy?' I look behind, and at the bottom of the steps there is a man standing there. He looks angry. The Walter man turns from me and looks at him. His expressions change; he seems to collapse from the inside. He's looking around him, and he takes a long drag on his cigarette.

'I said, are you with that boy?'

'Naa!' says Walter. 'I've never seen him before.'

'You sure?' continues the man, 'You seemed to be talking to him. Did you have you hand on his shoulders?'

'Oh that. Naa, he just asked if I would take him in to the pictures. I said naa – I was just telling him no.'

The man is still there. 'Lucky for you, Tweddle!' That's obviously Walter's name, 'Because if you were with him, and you were going to take him into the pictures, you know what would happen.'

'I wasn't taking him anywhere. I don't know the lad. I've just said no to him.'

The man looks at me, 'Was he taking you in to the film, son?'

'Him? No' I lie, 'I asked him, but he said no.'

'You are a lying little twat! I saw you walking down here. I've just followed you both. You came out of the Spanish City together!'

'No.' says Walter, 'he's telling the truth. I don't know him at all!'

The man is not convinced, and he has come closer to Walter, squaring up to him. 'The last time I saw you doing this, I told you what I would do to you, you piece of shit! Picking up young boys in the arcade and fiddling with them in the pictures. I warned you – I said what would happen!'

Walter is very frightened, he's dropped his cigarette, and seems to be sweating more than before.

The man turns to me, 'How kidda! Get yoursel away from here now, and divvent you come back! If I see you aroond here again, you'll be sorry! Go on – piss off. – and stay away from filthy twats like this man!'

I don't need to be told a second time. Off I go, down the steps. I'm going straight to the bus station - no detours, back home as soon as I can. I turn my head quickly as I reach the pavement, and I see the man pushing Walter into the side of the staircase and up against the wall.

A few yards up the road, I stop. I have to turn around and look back at the entrance to the Picture House. I see Walter still standing where I had left him. He has both hands up to his head when I see him, and then he begins to move gingerly down the steps.

He leans against one of the pillars, holding himself up with one hand and with the other he reaches into his pocket. I can see the blood on his face from here. His nose is a mess, and he finds something in his pocket to wipe his face, wincing as he tries to clean himself up. I don't see the man who has done this anywhere.

Part of me feels very bad about this. Walter was quite kind to me. He paid for me to play on the machines, and he was going to take me to the pictures. But as I look towards him now, he sees me staring at him.

He catches my eye, and the way that he then looks at me, a look of such intense anger and hatred, as he holds my stare for what seems forever, tells me that there is so much going on here, and that I understand hardly any of it.

I turn, and I run. I run all the way up to the bus station without stopping once, and when I get on to the number twelve to come home, I sit upstairs at the back of the bus, looking out of the window to make sure that Walter is not there. I do not see him; he has not followed me, and I make a promise to myself to keep away from the Spanish City, from the Regal cinema and from the Picture House, forever – a promise that, of course, I do not keep.

Fourteen
Plaza!!

'I assumed that everything must yield to me, that the entire universe had to flatter my whims, and that I had the right to satisfy them at will.' Marquis de Sade

So, there's me and Tommy Cox, and we're fifteen years old and pissed out of our minds on Front Street, Tynemouth. We are both palatic! – mortal! We've maybe had three or four pints – tomorrow we'll pretend it was eight, obviously – and it's about quarter past ten. Last orders will be called in about ten or fifteen minutes, so we've got to decide.

We've just left the Turk's Head and we're on our way to The Gib, (The Gibraltar Rock, but always known as the Gib) when Tommy shouts, 'Plazaaaaaaaa!'

A 'high risk strategy' is what we would call it today, but on that summer's evening in 1962, this option, being debated by a couple of drunken teenagers, was just one of several stupid next steps that we could have chosen, all of which were guaranteed to get us into trouble.

Tommy was my best mate, 'me marra'. We'd passed the eleven plus and we were both at THS (Tynemouth High School); neither of us particularly motivated to take advantage of the education being offered. We were much more interested in having a daft time, messing about, getting into trouble and the 'Plaza' option fitted the bill exactly.

The 'Plaza' – to which Tommy had just referred, was a huge building between Tynemouth and Cullercoats, across the road from the boating lake and overlooking the beach and the sea. I'm not sure what really went on there.

As I remember it, there was a skating rink outside, and there were bars and cafes, and an aquarium, I think. Was there also a wrestling arena? It burned down in the nineties, and I suppose I could look it up, but I can't be arsed. Anyway, our interest was in the dance – the Saturday night dance - and of course, any girls who might be found there.

I'm thinking back to that time now. I often think back to then, and when I do, apart from anything else, I never fail to be astonished at the confidence of it all.

We were just so bloody confident: confident in the expectation that when we eventually did roll up – anywhere, a party to which we were uninvited, a church hall social where a twitchy vicar would be weighing up his options from the moment we staggered through the door, we truly believed that the girls would be waiting to jump on us, to gratify us, to worship us – not that they ever did!

So, we set ourselves up to fail – again. Tommy's 'Plazaaaaaa!' meant that we would try to get in to the dance at the Plaza – if we could find a way of getting in. As I said, we'd already had three, maybe four pints each, and what with the packet of ten fags – Embassy - that was all our money spent. Our magnificent plan was for us to get there, about a fifteen-minute walk from where we now were, to see who was on the door, and if it wasn't anyone we knew, we'd find another way of getting in. It was that good a plan. Oh, and by the way, the idea that we might know one of the bouncers who would let us in was also high up in the realms of utter impossibility, alongside our expectation of the hordes of girls who would be dancing around their handbags, one eye on the door, awaiting our arrival.

There was quite a large crowd when we arrived, milling around, coming and going. Most of the people outside were much older than us – and some were much more aggressively drunk than we were, and the atmosphere was already electric, dangerous.

On a previous occasion, I had seen a very smartly dressed lad who had been refused entrance - since he was absolutely mortal too! - put his foot straight through a huge plate glass window. In comparison to these much older lads, we did look a bit young to be trying to get in to the dance this late in the evening. Maybe we would have got in more easily at eight or nine o'clock, but now would be pushing it.

Yet another challenge, but one that I now know was offset by the magic 'cloak of invincibility' that we both were proud of wearing.

Shoplifting the latest LPs (we called it 'flamming')? No problem – hide them under the cloak, and no-one will notice. Bunking off school of an afternoon? No problem – nobody will think it odd that a couple of THS schoolboys, wearing their classy, but rather distinctive school uniforms – bottle green jacket with yellow trimmings - are down the Spanish City playing the machines at two o'clock in the afternoon We tried to use the cloak now.

'Where're do you think you're going son?'

'In to the dance, man. Let us through...'

'Hold it. How old are you lads?'

'Eighteen.'

'F*** off! Come back when you are eighteen', the bouncer said. 'Maybe in about five or six years' time.' And he laughed. His mate laughed too.

Now neither Tommy nor I would say that we were particularly 'hard cases', although we had both practised that bandy-legged walk that most of the hard men around us seemed to use.

I wasn't particularly pleased with my version of the walk because my feet splay naturally and that, combined with forcing my knees out to the side as far as I could, didn't really work for me – still doesn't. I would have made a lousy cowboy – that and being allergic to horses, not that there were any horses outside the Plaza, just a couple of seriously threatening young men giving us the thousand-yard stare.

Tommy didn't want to let this go. He was comfortably surrounded by the cloak – and the confidence-boosting qualities conferred on him by three or four pints of Scotch. And he wanted to get in to the dance. After all, we had walked a long way, and if we didn't get in there'd be nothing else we could do.

'Listen man, Haway! We're both eighteen – we've already been in! We had to come out just before, and now we want to get back in....'

The bouncer looked at us. 'Where's your stamp? Show us your wrists, canny lad.'

'Me Stamp? There was no time for a stamp, man! It's me lass's purse – it's had all her money in it. Her pay packet and everything.' Tommy had found his theme. 'Me girlfriend thought she had left her purse in the Clachan bar back at the Grand. We've just been back to look for it. Hawaay man, let us back in! We've already paid once!'

'Where's the purse, then? Show me the purse.' Was this a chink of light?

'Naa – it wasn't there, man – or some twat nicked it before I got back to the Clachan.' (The Clachan Bar at the side of the Grand Hotel was the nearest bar to where we now were.)

If there had been a chink of light, it now was snuffed out. 'I've told you to f*** off once, lad. Do I have to tell youse again?'

Tommy pulled the cloak tighter round himself as he squared up to the bouncer.

'Oh yeah! And what are you going to do about it, you big twat? I'll f****** ploat you if you try!' Tommy had warmed to his theme now. He was living his dream as a combination of our cloak of invincibility and the stimulus of a few pints of beer took him into the unknown.

'Ploating' is what we talked about a lot. 'I'll f****** ploat you' is what we said to each other if we were mildly annoyed. We hadn't used that term with a bouncer before, as far as I was aware. As I said earlier, we were operating a high-risk strategy, and sometimes you win and sometimes.....

This time we lost. Both of us – we both lost! Nowadays most doormen outside pubs and clubs have been on a course. Most doormen are licensed. They don't have criminal records mostly - either, and they pride themselves on their customer service. It's fair to say that the two bouncers we were so loudly confronting hadn't been on any course. It's also fair to say, on reflection, that they probably welcomed the arrival of a couple of mouthy teenage yobs to liven up their evening.

It's over fifty years since that night, and things mellow somewhat over time. I now think that I might have used some tactic other than drunken confrontation. I might have approached the situation differently. I also have my own ideas of what should have been done were I the bouncer in question on that evening so very, very long ago.

But let me ask you. It's possible that we might be on a similar wavelength.   What would you have done if you were a big, muscular lad, employed to look after the door of a dance hall on a Saturday night? What would you have done when Tommy and I decided to swear at you and threaten to 'f****** ploat' you?

Yes, Exactly! First Tommy, and then me. The bouncer moved one step towards Tommy, grabbed his lapels and nutted him. Tommy sank to the floor like a limp rag. I had time only to see the first part of this process before the explosion went off in my head and I too was collapsing to the floor.

Not wishing to waste an opportunity, the other bouncer had joined in, and a second loudmouthed teenager outside that dance hall had found that his cloak of invincibility wasn't quite fit for purpose.

The bridge of my nose and my right eye were sore for ages, and the bruising took weeks to fade. Over time, Tommy and I concocted separate tales - but curiously similar – about how we were jumped on by two, no - three much older lads outside the Plaza. Yes, we both said in our own way, this looks bad, but you should have seen the other guys!

And that was the highlight of the evening. A night to remember. At least, I certainly remember it. We didn't get into the dance, didn't even see, never mind score with any girls, and to top it all off, when we eventually staggered back to Tommy's house – up near Billy Mill - to try and clean ourselves up, Tommy's mother, standing by the window in the front room, but in the dark, watched me as I relieved myself into her carefully tended rose bushes.

Fifteen
Driving in the right direction?

'Fat, drunk and stupid is no way to go through life, boy' Dean Wormer, Animal House,1978

I have five children, two girls and three boys, and for them learning to drive a car has been simply a rite of passage, something that you do. Come seventeen, the driving lessons begin. When you are ready, you take a test. If you are one of my daughters, you pass first time – as did their mother. If you are one of my sons, you fail – as did their father, and you must try again, and keep trying, until you pass.

Once having passed the test, the car you drive just becomes a means of getting around. You might polish it once or twice to begin with, but then you realise that you can't be bothered; it's another piece of stuff. You buy, lease or hire one, or you get a vehicle with your job. Simple, uncomplicated and unruffled.

Not so with me, the obsessive! I start driving cars from about the age of thirteen. It is four years until I can take my driving test, and probably once or twice every day from then on, I think of the moment that I will get my green slip. Pathetic but true.

I think about getting a job at weekends – preferably so I can be near engines and cars. Maybe if I work in a garage, I can learn more about vehicles? I also consider leaving school to become an apprentice mechanic, or for any other kind of job that might be car related.

Jobs are hard to get. There's not much on offer for a thirteen-year-old lad with an 'attitude problem' as Mam calls it. I could deliver newspapers, but I've never wanted to be a paper boy, as I am no good at getting up in the morning. I was slightly tempted recently because a lad I know has started stealing cigarettes from the newspaper shop where he works, and he sells them in singles to boys at school.

He is making a lot of money, he tells me, but he's bound to get caught. He's flamming packs of two hundred each time now because his business is so good – too many to get away with for any length of time – and he's bragging about it too. I would have thought he'd be more sensible keeping quiet.

There is another way I could make money from cigarettes, and I have tried it once or twice, but it is scary. This way would involve me making regular visits to the Fish Quay, preferably at night – and that's the main reason why I choose not to carry on doing it.

There are many foreign fishing boats that tie up at the quay, and the men who work on them, particularly the deep sea trawlermen, always seem to have cigarettes to sell. So, the Fish Quay is the place. I have learned a bit of German, and it seems to work even if the trawlermen are from other countries like Poland or Norway.

What you do is walk next to one of the trawlers and when you see a man on the deck, you say, 'Haben sie zigaretten verkaufen, bitte?' If the answer is yes, you then say 'Wie viel?' That means 'How much?' Then he tells you – usually it is two quid, and you can buy a pack of two hundred tabs, or more if you have the cash.

It sounds easy enough, and it is. But I have heard stories that make me worry. I don't believe the ones about young lads disappearing on to the trawlers never to be seen again. I have always known of those stories but have never known of a single boy who has disappeared.

But the ones about the police arresting people for smuggling - I do know about those, and they are true. Just a few weeks ago, four men who were caught smuggling were sent to prison, and the papers made it into a huge story. The thought of going to prison for buying a few tabs? That's not for me.

However, if you do manage not to be caught, a box of ten packets of Chesterfields or Lucky Strikes can be sold on at a shilling a tab. That can generate a profit of six or eight pounds - and give you a couple of packs for yourself - if you are prepared to take the risk and spend a lot of time selling them.

We are really struggling for money at home because my mam is having to bring up the four of us by herself. The insurance company did not pay out on my dad's life policy because he killed himself, so she did not receive the five hundred pounds that she expected.

She now goes out to work every day, and puts Marion and Patricia, now aged two and three, into the nursery at the bottom of Cleveland Road.

Before she had children, Mam worked as a shorthand typist, so after Dad died, and she had to go back to work, she looked around and got a job working at a solicitor's office in Northumberland Square. She has just passed some exams and is now a 'legal executive'; she has her own office next door to her boss, Mr Potts – but we are still very short of money.

One of the reasons for this is that we have moved out of our council house on the Marden – too many unhappy memories for Mam, I think.

First, we lived for a short while in York Terrace on Coach Lane, and now we've recently moved to a house that Mam has been able to buy.

Mr Potts helped her to get a mortgage, and we moved from Stanton Road, first to the house in York Terrace and then to where we now live, number sixteen, Alma Place.

With the mortgage and the nursery fees taking up so much of my mam's pay – and her not receiving that five hundred pounds from the insurance company - money I think she was relying on, Mam has nothing to spare for me.

I say that's ok, I'll get myself a job. She reminds me that I am only thirteen years old. I say that my dad left school at thirteen and started working for an organ maker. Her reply is that times are different now, and the new law will require me to stay on at school until I am sixteen – but she wants me to stay on for two extra years and do my A levels.

I know she worries: she says if I get a job, my school work will be affected. I know that's true, but I want to have money to spend. We had a huge row about it, of course, and I won - as is usual now.

I am just too big and too noisy for her to control me, and I like that. I said that I would get a job. Part of me just wants to help her manage a little better, but the other part of me wants to make sure that I get my own way. The second part won – again.

It's not just work, though. I need to get out of the house at night, and since I stopped going to the Gang Shows, I have been enjoying sport. I was never any good at football, but I have had some success at rugby, so much so that I join Percy Park rugby club hoping to be their new sensational wing forward.

The current hero at 'Park' is Don Rutherford, the full back who has just been selected to play for England. And I train with Don Rutherford. Well, I don't exactly train with him, I go to Percy Park on the same nights that he trains.

Of course, I never speak to him, never receive a pass or try to pass to him, but I watch him from afar and quickly realise that I have absolutely no chance of doing very well at this game. It's like me with football – I have tremendous enthusiasm, but I am too slow, too clumsy – and an absolute chicken when it comes to tackling. My regard for myself as a rugby player diminishes by the moment.

However, on the networking front, going to a few training sessions and getting some games in the Percy Park fourth team is a great success. I find out that a man called Hewitt, who also plays there, owns a service station and garage in Chirton Village.

He's John Hewitt, and I'm told that he was a very skilled fly half in his younger days. He now captains the third team, and that is the team which turns out to be the zenith of my rugby-playing career. I play two games in the thirds - never to be reselected again. But I do play with John Hewitt. John has been a first team player for many years, and there is a certain tragic quality to his now having to play with the likes of me if he wants to get a game, but he is still very enthusiastic – and really fast!

I am soon convinced that any thoughts that I might have of being a decent rugby player have turned to ashes, but it's not Don Rutherford, or even his brother Maurice, with whom I do play once, who sets me straight on this score. It's John Hewitt, a man of forty-odd who can still glide past an opponent like a ghost, and who, in our sprinting sessions, is still twice as fast as me – yet you hardly ever see him off the pitch without a cigarette in his mouth.

That grey county cap with its red tassel and piping is never going to happen but playing a couple of games with Mr Hewitt – and getting to call him 'John' transforms my chances of getting the job I have been looking for.

I know it's bad form, but during a game one Saturday afternoon, when I am playing at wing forward, and he at fly half, I ask him if I can have a job on a Sunday – and he says yes, come around tomorrow morning and we will see what can be done – this conversation makes him lose concentration for a moment, and he is rewarded by being flattened with a thumping great tackle.

***

I have been working at his garage in Chirton for just over a year. No spare money at home means that if I want something like a new pair of jeans or a shirt for myself, I must work to earn it. I know that I am still a kid, and that I am at the High School and should be making the most of my opportunities, but if I want to look smart when I go out with my mates, I need money.

John Hewitt's job turns out to be great choice for me. It's legal – no smuggling involved, although it's probably not legal for Mr Hewitt to employ me as I am only thirteen when I start. He pays me in cash, and I earn enough each week to buy my clothes. I can also help my mam a bit, and something I never thought of - I learn to drive for free.

Marco is the mechanic at the garage, and he services the cars. He only works on weekdays, and sometimes cars are left at the garage for Marco to start on when he comes in on a Monday morning. I work on Sundays

– sometimes Saturdays too – so there are often cars left on the forecourt over the weekend, and the keys are hung on hooks right next to the till. Two or three other vehicles are always there on the forecourt. Those cars are for sale, but nobody seems to be interested in buying them.

I first learn to drive by getting the keys for one of these cars from the hook, starting the car, and then going up and down the forecourt. There is not enough room for me to change gear, so on the forecourt, I can only drive in first – and reverse. Soon I become a little more daring, and I change my plan.

Now, if I drive down Lilburn Street, turn the corner and then drive back up Silkey's Lane, I can drive quite fast. I try this, first in the bottle green Rover 80, and then in the big, black Austin Sixteen, two cars that are always here – and I can get into third gear in both of them quite easily. I decide that I prefer the Rover, but the Austin is much faster in first and second gear.

Each Sunday afternoon, when the pumps are quiet, and I am getting bored, I get the keys of whichever cars have been left over the weekend and I go for a drive around the block, or if there are no customers' cars, I take the Rover or the Austin.

Of course, I do want to be able to drive legally, but that can't happen until I am seventeen. When I pass my test, the first thing that I will do is buy a car. Before then, before I am seventeen, I have decided to get a motorbike, and I know at least one way how I can do that for free.

You can ride a motorbike when you are sixteen, and there is a job you can get that gives you one for your work - Post Office Telegram Boy! You get a uniform, a BSA 125 bike, and your belt has a pouch on it for the telegrams. I suggested to my mam that I leave school at sixteen and get a job as a telegram boy, but she just laughed. I don't know why, it looks a great job.

Or, I could become a police driver. I also suggest that to my mam. She said that would be a good job, but she wants me to finish school first. She says that I should go into the sixth form, but I think that I will earn more money if I leave school at sixteen.

This love I have for cars is not new, it stretches right back. When I was about six or seven, and living on the Marden, Mr Mackay, Nigel's dad, bought the first car on our part of Hartington Road. It was a green Riley Pathfinder with a black roof. He was very proud of that car – and of all the attention it, and he, received.

The car itself fascinated people: our neighbours - the men mostly, would cluster around it talking knowledgeably about its features, making comparisons with other cars that they knew. Some of the neighbours' children, all my friends, got to have a ride in it around the block. I never did ride in it – even though Nigel and I played together almost every day. My dad didn't like Mr Mackay for some reason, and I am not sure that Mr Mackay liked him.

And one other car – I've always called it the 'magic one'. Just to sit in it, that's all I wanted – nothing else. I still dream about it today.

This is how the magic car came into my life. One morning, on the corner of Hartington Road and Wallington Avenue, parked, not on the road itself, but on a strip of grass between the road and the pavement, there appeared overnight the most amazing bright yellow American Buick Riviera sedan. It was huge – it was twice the size of any car I had ever seen before. It was so different, so – American, with long tail fins and chrome everywhere.

As well as the startlingly garish colour, remember we were living in black and white then, it also had dark green tinted windows, a massive steering wheel with a chrome inner circle for the horn, and the most outrageous chromium grille that looked just like the teeth of one of the scary dragons in my favourite story book. Fabulous whitewall tyres and shiny silver spoke wheels completed the dream.

I just looked at it - hypnotised by it and all that it represented of a world beyond my imagination. Ever since then I have dreamed that it's mine, that I am the guy driving it – 'getting my kicks' down the fabled Route 66 – where that car truly belongs.

My right arm is draped around the shoulders of my adoring blonde girlfriend who is sitting up close to me on the bench seat (remember them?) her head nestled on my shoulder. The stereo is up to eleven – perfecting the image (Yes, I know. I've allowed some creative latitude there, with the stereo – and the blonde!).

For years, I had a picture of that Buick on my bedroom wall. My Uncle Tom had also seen the car, and he had also seen how it mesmerised me. One day, he brought me a copy of an American car magazine – and there was my Buick in its startling yellow and green colour scheme. That double page picture – not a photo, but a coloured drawing, became my first 'centrefold', and it stayed on my bedroom wall until we moved to a new house.

This apparition visits our planet for only about three or four days; it allows me to stand next to it and, in my own way, I am permitted to worship it. Then it disappears, never to return. Later I find out that it belongs to an American soldier who has brought his war bride back home to visit her family. I never see either of them, but I loved that car – and still do.

One day I will have that Buick – and the girlfriend. But now I must be contented with my plans for a motorbike - and with the joys of Pauline across the road.

Because here is a surprise – at least it has come as a surprise to me. Over the last few months, the eczema that has been with me all through my childhood has disappeared. My skin is now clear, and especially at the back of my legs and the insides of my elbows, there is no itching at all. There are no keens on the joints of my fingers either - it's as if my eczema was never there.

Girls have always been repulsed by my dry, flaky skin, and when I was in the primary school and I had to wear shorts all the time, lots of kids, the girls especially, would react if ever I accidentally touched them, by squealing and pretending to be sick – worried that they might catch some sort of disease from me.

All that has changed: I find that I appear to be quite attractive to girls now. At least, they react more pleasantly to me.

Across the road from the garage, there is a girl called Pauline who sits and looks out of the window at me whenever I am working. She watches me as I fill cars the with fuel and oil, or I repair punctures and change wheels. (I also find out sometime later that she is doing the same thing when my pal Ian is working on a different shift, but that is a story for another time.)

One day, after I finish work, I clean my hands with the Swarfega, tidy myself up as much as I can, and I walk over the road to her house. She invites me in and we both go upstairs together – not to a bedroom, but to where she looks out of the window at me. Her flat is on the first floor; I never see her bedroom.

For months and months after I first meet Pauline, I go upstairs to her family's flat after I finish work. Her parents are sometimes in, sometimes not, but I never meet either of them. I might see them coming and going from their front door, but they never acknowledge me, and I never speak to them.

On reflection, the other curious thing is that Pauline and I never meet under any other circumstances. I never take her out to the pictures, never even go for a walk with her as far as I can remember. No, all

Pauline wants is for me (and it seems, Ian) to visit her when we finish work. So – we do.

***

This new life I am starting to lead produces a complete reordering of my priorities. At the top of the list I place earning money – mostly from working at the garage at the weekend – and the occasional evening shift too. Over one Easter holiday, and with another girlfriend called Alison, I get almost two weeks' worth of employment with a company called Mass Observation, counting how many cars travel up and down the Coast Road – and being paid for it.

And alongside my regular job at the garage, I have picked up a few others. One is on the Tyne Commissioners' Quay where the Bergen Line and its ships Venus and Leda as well as the Fred Olsen Cruises, embark passengers for Norway. My job is as one of the group of porters, boys, all selected on the day – no regular employment arrangements here – who either load or unload passengers' luggage. This involves delivering suitcases to the cabins and generally helping to carry anything on or off the ship that needs to be carried.

We start very early, normally about six in the morning, and I am finished for about eight. Sometimes I get to school a bit late. I manage to keep that job until I am sacked immediately when I stupidly announce that I have been able to get yet another job, this time with the Tyne Brand factory on the Fish Quay.

I get work as a general labourer in a factory that produces tinned foods – Tyne Brand Stuffed Pork Roll, Tyne Brand Minced Beef with Onion and the best of all, Tyne Band Steak and Kidney Pie. This means that all my holidays are taken up with work, as are most of my weekends and sometimes two or three evenings a week.

I get other labouring jobs too. I work with a building contractor laying the road that links The Tyne Tunnel with the Coast Road; that job lasts for four or five weeks one summer. I also spend two very painful weeks breaking up hard core for the foundations of a school that will soon be built in Wallsend.

I remember that my dad had a whole series of jobs, but I think that I have outdone him – and I am still at school.

Girls - and getting palatic (very drunk) - also rate high on my new priorities, and with all the money I earn, I can indulge myself in both. I now seem to spend very little time at home, becoming more and more distant from both my mam who is aware of my descent into a hell of my own making.

My sisters come to see their big brother, not as the father figure that I am sure they would wish, but more as the unpleasant stranger who seems always to be arguing with their mother.

With the money I earn, and over a period of fifteen weeks, I pay a bloke one pound a week – each Friday night when he comes to put some petrol in his car. After ten weeks, he brings me the object of my desire – something that I have been buying on an informal kind of 'hire purchase' agreement.

I now own my first set of 'wheels'. I have bought and almost paid for an 'Adler' motor scooter. I have not told my mother yet, but it is taxed and insured, and I already have a provisional licence entitling me to ride it. My new scooter is blue and shiny – it's quite old – but the man says that it is much better than either the Vespa or the Lambretta scooters that we see everywhere.

My first motoring tragedy: this scooter is a disaster! It has an electric starter than never works: twice in the first week it suddenly cuts out when I am riding it, and I have to push it home.

The next Friday, when the bloke comes for his money, I tell him about the scooter, and that I want my money back. He laughs. He then says if I don't pay him the rest of his money as agreed, he will 'fill me in'. This particular sale it seems, doesn't come with a money back guarantee.

Whenever my scooter does stutter into life, and I get the opportunity to ride it, I never venture too far from home as I am aware that I may well have to push it back. So, while the engine is running, I tend to go uphill, rather than down. This means that showing my new wheels off on Front Street, Tynemouth is a risky endeavour, and not worth either the effort or the humiliation of pushing the damn thing all the way back up to North Shields if, as I am sure it will, it conks out on me.

And its major fault is that it's not a car. Yes, it's true that I can get to some places more easily - if I don't go uphill. But I can only go by myself. The thing has only one seat – something I should really have noticed before I bought it.

And my main wish is to be able to take a girl with me – preferably to somewhere dark and quiet. Or maybe to pick up my mates and take them all out to a country pub. None of this is possible with my scooter and anyway, I'm not giving quite the impression that I had hoped. The Adler is very slow, very loud, and of course, I never know when it is going to break down on me.

And still my mother doesn't know anything about it! Our house is on a corner, so our yard has a narrow alley leading to it from the back lane.

Nobody uses the back-lane entrance, so my scooter stays there, in the little lane, and remains my secret. I suppose that I should tell Mam sometime – after all, people have seen me riding it, and somebody is bound to mention it to her, but I persist in trying to keep it a secret.

***

Right at the bottom of the list of my priorities, layered over with the meretricious arguments that justify me choosing to drive cars and motorbikes, to work at many different jobs, to drink beer with my mates, to go out with girls whenever I can, and to buy as many clothes as I need - comes the truly important aspect of my life, the aspect that is suffering the 'death of a thousand cuts': my education.

The choices I have made so far are all plausible; I am plausible – to myself - but it turns out that simply put, I am paying no attention, giving no time, to getting an education.

There is a point to being a child – a value in moving from childhood, through adolescence and into maturity at a measured pace – and I am missing that point entirely. I want it all now. There are no constraining influences suggesting that I wait a while, suggesting that I prepare myself for my adult life – no, I know exactly what being an adult involves, and I won't hear anybody telling me otherwise.

Today, the real adult in me thinks that it is very healthy that a child learns the discipline of working for an employer quite early in life. In my own family, all my children have had jobs while they were at school, and we encouraged that. We did so because we knew that we could keep this in control, and that the main thrust of adolescence should be that of preparing for the world of work, and nowadays, the most important route: that of university.

It is different for me. I decide how and when I will work to earn money, and my choices simply ignore any value that there might be in deferred gratification. I want it now – as much of everything that I can have – immediately.

The result of what turn out to be my stupid choices means that I am not able to keep up with the work at school. I don't read enough, never finish my homework, and if I do, I never get it in on time. Although somewhere in my stupid head the little voice is telling me that I should be re-ordering things in my life, I simply don't listen to it.

My GCE results are dreadful, and not nearly good enough to allow me passage into the sixth form. This time last year I would have been delighted by this. I would have been happy to have left school, maybe even as an Easter leaver, and I could now be working at Tyne Brand and earning a full-time wage.

But maybe my stupid head has been listening; maybe I have been absorbing at least some of what that little voice has been shouting at me. I have decided that staying on at school might be a good thing after all.

The Saturday morning after the GCE results come out, I go cap in hand, to Mr Cantle (always known as 'Albert') the headmaster, who also happens to live in Alma Place. I ask if I can be given the opportunity to come in to the sixth form, even though my results are terrible.

To be fair to the man, he possibly sees potential in me that few others have seen so far, and he agrees to put me on probation. If I can prove myself during the first few weeks of next term, I will be allowed to join the sixth form – six weeks after everybody else, but I will also have to retake some of my GCEs - and pass them, if I am to be allowed to stay on at school.

It's the best – the only deal I can get, and I accept it. On my way back home, a walk of about two or three hundred yards, I immediately discount the deal, and I go back to thinking about my true priorities – girls, booze, and now that I am nearing my seventeenth birthday – driving cars and more specifically, the driving test itself.

Because my birthday is in the middle of September, I am at school - still on probation - when I apply to take my driving test.

I don't have a car of my own, and nobody else in the family has one that I could borrow. The only driving lessons I have ever had are the ones that I have given myself by driving round and round the houses of Chirton Village. Even that has had to stop because somebody has complained to Mr Hewitt and said that if it continued, they would go to the police. None of us owned up to anything, and Mr Hewitt threatened to sack us all if anything like this happened again.

Now all the car keys are locked away each night and over weekends. Ken, the old bloke who is in charge of everything when Mr Hewitt is not around, has received instructions – and he now obeys those instructions to the letter.

My date for the driving test is the last week of September, and I decide to buy a copy of the Highway Code. I try to do some revision - probably better to say some reading – as revision implies that you may have already read it. Also, in desperation, I ask Mr Hewitt if I can be allowed to borrow a car for the driving test.

I do have to paint a bleak picture, poverty-stricken mother etc, but he reluctantly agrees. My test is at eleven o'clock on a Tuesday morning – a school day – and he agrees to meet me outside the school on that morning.

At about ten thirty, I leave school to meet Mr Hewitt. I am still wearing school uniform. Sixth formers can wear whatever clothes they like, but I am still on probation; still officially a fifth former. This is truly ironic as I have great clothes that I would love to wear, but I can't wear them at school.

The car is waiting for me. It is a Ford Cortina; white, and it looks quite new. The person driving it is not Mr Hewitt, but Mr Hewitt's current girlfriend, Carole. She doesn't like me very much because I know what has happened to her.

She disappeared for about three weeks, and when she returned she told me, one evening last week, that she had been away to 'lose a bit of weight'. She has lost weight, that is true, and although I am just seventeen, I know exactly how she lost it, and she knows that I know! And that is why she doesn't like me.

She smiles a very forced smile, says hello and asks me if I would like to drive the car to the test centre in North Shields 'for a bit of practice'.

That seems like a good idea as I have never driven a car with a passenger before, so I say yes and get into the driver's seat. The engine is running: Carole has not switched it off while waiting for me. She then explains why.

The battery is flat. If I do switch it off – or if I stall the engine – we won't be able to start it again. We set off from school and turn right at the traffic lights and drive down Queen Alexandra Road. I am a bit worried about stalling, and at the lights at the bottom where we turn right again, I am very careful. Driving past Preston Hospital, I am starting to feel quite confident, although I have only ridden my motorbike in traffic before.

When we get to the driving test centre, just off Northumberland Square, I park in the road, apply the handbrake, and leave the engine running while I go in to find the examiner.

So far, so good. The examiner is waiting for me, and once we are outside, he asks me to read a car number plate from twenty-five yards, which I am able to do without difficulty.

He sees Carole sitting in 'my' car, and he politely asks her to come out of the vehicle and wait inside the centre until we return. He then gets into the passenger front seat and waits for me to get into the driver's side.

The first thing he asks me to do is to start the vehicle. The engine is already running, so I engage first gear, click the indicator and look carefully into the mirror.

He stops me and, once again, he asks me to start the engine. I point out that the engine is already running. He tells me that he is aware of that, but the first requirement of the driving test is that the driver 'start the vehicle'.

I explain to him that if I do switch the engine off, it will not start again. That is not his problem, he tells me, and asks me, once again, to start the engine.

I am panicking now because I know exactly what will happen next. I won't be able to start the car, and I doubt whether he will help me to bump start it again.

I switch the engine off, crossing my fingers as I turn the key. Nothing! The engine won't even turn over; there is no life in the battery. I'm already thinking of how we are going to get it back to the garage at Chirton.

The examiner fills out a form – it's not the green slip that I had hoped for, but the dreaded pink one that tells me I have failed, and which also tells me that I must find a way to keep this disaster secret. Obviously, I can't tell my mates that I have been given a pink slip – only losers get the pink slip!

The examiner explains, quite formally, that I have not met the standard required for me to be recognised as a competent driver, and that accordingly, I have failed the test. The reason: 'failed to start the vehicle'. He looks at me, says Good Morning, and as he gets out of the car, I detect the beginnings of a smile. I guess that his early coffee break is going to be enriched with a new war story.

Carole comes out of the test centre and looks at me. I know my place. I get out from the driver's seat and I walk round to the back of the car, ready to start pushing. Carole releases the hand brake and the car starts to move – purely by chance it is parked facing down the slight hill – and the vehicle begins to gain momentum.

She has obviously practised this manoeuvre before because as she engages second gear and lets out the clutch, the car sparks into life – and off she goes! She neither stops to pick me up, nor does she turn around and come back up the hill. I assume that she is going back to

Chirton, and I begin the sad, slow walk up to the High School and to the realisation that I am beginning to fail most things in a pretty big way.

That was my driving opportunity – and I failed to grasp it. Did that kick me into reality? Was that the Damascene moment? Yes, in a couple of ways, it was. I never return to the garage at Chirton, and I stop playing rugby at Percy Park.

But apart from those minor changes, no, I don't think so. My stupidity was so ingrained that it would take a lot more to get me to change direction. Any radical shift from this trajectory had to come from a different source. It would not be outside events that shaped my thinking towards a more mature world view, it had to come from within.

And it did. I discover that the sixth form gives me levels of responsibility and excitement that I have never had before. I meet a truly inspirational couple of teachers who get me to want to develop my mind. I come to see how I intuitively 'understand' Theatre, and I develop a deep love for literature both in English and French. Having an immense crush on my new A Level English teacher helps me concentrate my mind wonderfully too!

I discover that I have a minor talent for acting, and suddenly much of my stupidity seems to fall away. I get involved in school productions as a stage manager. My English teacher mentions the National Youth Theatre to me in conversation, and I eventually get to play minor roles in a number of its productions.

I now know that I am never going to be a great sportsman, but I know that I will be able to play for enjoyment, and that turns out to be enough for me. I play in the first fifteen rugby teams for two years, and I also find myself in the first eleven cricket team – more due to a paucity of talent in our school than in any particular ability of mine. However, I am now able to accept that in some things I am doomed to be mediocre, and that I had better start concentrating on those things that I might be able to do well.

I still like drinking and going out with my mates, but my obsessive behaviours moderate, and I start to work at school – developing my mind and getting the education that I know I need. Slowly my list of priorities, while not entirely changing, starts to see education as being the key to my escaping from North Shields, and that becomes my main objective – escape!

I don't pass my driving test for another two years. Somehow it seems much less important. What did St Paul say? 'Childish things?' He was right, and when I put them away, I think I became a better man.

Sixteen
The Backdrop to these Stories

'Once you get there, you find there is no 'there' Gertrude Stein

I am naturally hoping that people who know nothing of me will have enjoyed reading these stories, and to you I would say this: if there is a point, and obviously, I think that I have written this for a purpose, it is primarily to show to my kids, my grandkids and to anyone else who is thinking of bringing children into this world, how important is the influence of parents and role models in the shaping of a child's future. Charles Martin says, *'Never judge someone by their relatives.'* I would love to agree with him, and I hope that most of us try not to be too judgmental, or to categorise people into stereotypes.

After reading some of these stories, you will be challenged not to draw conclusions about my relatives. In some of these stories, it is the negative that will make the point. In others, I hope you see the positives that can come from the influence of strong role models.

'Events, dear boy, events.' as a prime minister once said, conspired to create circumstances where our parents' lives were wrenched out of their control. Consequently, we their children, lost our childhoods very quickly – this despite our mother's brave attempt to carry on after the early death of our father.

There were four children in my immediate family, and we were all affected in different ways. I was the oldest child and the only boy. My early life was 'casebook' typical of a young man without a father – too much freedom and too many distractions – some of those distractions verging on criminality.

My college and university education – plus my marriage to a very strong woman – allowed me the possibility of redemption, which I grasped. Together, Wendy and I have had five children. They are all making their way successfully in the world, and as I write, it appears that they are all in secure personal relationships and pursuing demanding, but very exciting careers.

I hope that I am not tempting Fate too much, and I know that the saying is 'If you want to make God laugh, you tell him your plans'. Wendy and I have never tried to make plans for our children – neither have we been living our lives vicariously through their achievements. But they all know that we wanted them to set high expectations for themselves, and we were there to support them in achieving their objectives.

For example, leaving school at sixteen was not an option for our kids. All, bar one, went willingly to university and achieved master's degrees and more. The one whose arm was twisted started university but chose not to stay. Nevertheless, he is now a well read and truly rounded adult. His education was slightly eccentric, as was mine, but he is very competent in his work and, more importantly, he now is a great dad.

One way or another, our children have all seen the benefit and the value of a good education. My wife and I have noticed that those who are parents have already started to process of encouragement that leads to the setting of high expectations for their children.

It must have been obvious to you – after reading the stories, that I wish that I had had the space and time during my adolescence to reflect more sensibly about any next steps that I was about to take. I have spent my life trying to compensate and catching up.

The same must be said for my siblings, my three sisters. Their childhoods were full of stress from the time that our father died, and it has taken many years for us all to feel 'comfortable' with life, and in the case of one of my sisters, such a state has never happened.

My eldest sister Glenda, when aged sixteen, escaped the family as soon as she could by joining the army and becoming a nurse. She married Robert, also in the army, and had two sons. In later life, however, she was able to study theology at St Andrews, obtain her MA, and become an ordained minister in the Presbyterian Church of Scotland.

That career change was made because she eventually found that she had 'choice' – something that she ought to have had earlier in her life, but which was snuffed out by the impossibility of her then home situation.

My sister Marion was passing through early adolescence when our mother died and was only about one year old at the death of our father. She too trained to become a nurse. Her marriage to Shaun has been a great success, and they have two children.

I think that life was difficult for Marion before she met Shaun, but her natural kindness, and her very own kind of resilience has allowed her too to become stronger at dealing with the challenges that beset us all.

Patricia is my youngest sister, and it is difficult to know what to write about her because I must confess that I don't know her as well as I should.

She was about thirteen when our mother died. I was working in Switzerland at the time, and I resigned my job to move back to the UK. We already had our two oldest children by now, and we had thoughts of bringing Marion and Patricia to live with us.

In the meantime, my friend Alex took in Marion to live with his family, and my mother-in-law, Jean, was happy to invite Patricia to live with her until our return.

The plan did not work out for my youngest sister, and by the time we could return to the UK with our daughter Melissa, and our new baby son, Jake, Patricia was in the care of the local authority, it having proved impossible to assimilate her into my wife's family.

Patricia lived in various foster homes after that, and then she became pregnant. Her daughter Lisa was born, and later Kathryn came along.

It soon became apparent that Patricia was unable to look after her two children. She suffered from a form of depression that made being a mother very challenging. I am certain that the experiences of her early years had simply not prepared her for parenthood.

I think that it is fair to say – but it is subjective, of course, that we, as a family, have done as much as we could to help. Most significantly, when Lisa was about ten years old, and Kathryn was seven, we brought the two girls into our family to live with us. As we had five children of our own by now, we needed a big house for the nine of us. Luckily, we were living at Allan Bank in Grasmere, and that proved to be the most marvellous place to bring up children.

We officially became foster parents for Patricia's two girls, and the arrangement worked well for Lisa until she was sixteen. At that age, and for various reasons, she chose to return to the care system. We kept in close touch with her; she went on to university, and now she has a degree and a post-graduate qualification. She is a great mum to her son Arran, and once again, Lisa is very much one of us. She and Arran are always an integral part of all our family occasions.

Kathryn, I think it is fair to say, tolerated living with us, but at the age of eighteen, she exercised her right as an adult to go back to live with her mother, Patricia.

Kathryn has become the carer for her mum, and if she is happy doing that, I am prepared to be happy for her.

***

This back story needs further digging to put it truly in its place. Going down the line to the previous generation is necessary, so please forgive me if this next short section reads like one of those odd books of the Old Testament – all that begetting and so on, but my great grandmother did have eight children. Here goes.

Agnes Ogilvie, my 'Granny', was born in Oldmeldrum, near Aberdeen in 1865, but her father, George, brought his family from Scotland to Barrow in Furness where he found work in the shipyards as an engine driver. Agnes appears in the 1881 census as living in Devonshire Buildings, just over the bridge on Walney Island, and is recorded, at the age of fifteen, as being a 'jute worker'.

She was eighteen when she married John Blain, a foreman plater from Hull who had also come to Barrow in search of work in the yards. Their first son, born in 1885, one year after they married, combined both of their names. He was christened 'George Ogilvie Blain'. Sadly, George died at the age of two. Thereafter, although Agnes' subsequent children were all christened, each was given only one Christian name – no middle names at all from then on.

Their youngest daughter, also Agnes, died from tuberculosis in her early thirties. Their eldest surviving son, James, emigrated to Vancouver Island, and had three children. Times were different then, and that part of the family was never to be seen again.

By the time of the 1901 census, the family had moved to North Shields and they were living at 55 Stormont Street. The other five siblings, Charlotte, Isabella, Elizabeth, Jane and Agnes, known as 'Aggie' plus the youngest son, John had also moved to Tyneside with their parents. Aggie, the youngest girl, died and John never married, but the remaining four girls found themselves husbands and settled down to married life. Those four marriages only produced a total of two children. One was Margaret, Isabella's girl, and the other was Jane's daughter, Agnes, who became my mam.

John Blain had moved to North Shields from Barrow, chasing work in the shipyards, but suffered a catastrophic stroke which left him completely paralysed. He died just before the outbreak of the war in 1939.

John was the main breadwinner for the family, and so that she could manage to care for her husband and feed her family, my great grandma converted the downstairs of their house in Stormont Street into corner shop.

In 1941, that shop was deemed so vital to the success of the British economy that the Luftwaffe decided to bomb it. That last sentence is not entirely true; it became collateral damage in an air raid on the Tyneside shipyards. A church nearby received a direct hit, and many houses all around were destroyed.

A Dr Martin offered the now homeless family a house of his at number four, Wallsend Road, and the remaining four, Granny, Grandma and Grandad and my great uncle John, moved there. No wonder Agnes took to her bed when she arrived at Wallsend Road and never came out of her room again. I think that I would have done the same thing.

All families are weird, I get that. And I know that I was growing up in a family that for the most part was already old. They were all locked in to an elderly mindset; they did not laugh - probably could not laugh, they had no kids to play with, and they all were seriously averse to risk taking of any kind.

Apart from Jane and Isabella, none of them had any children. Indeed, one of the husbands, Billy, my great aunt Bess's man, was diagnosed with something then known as 'nervous debility'. It was Dr Martin who offered the diagnosis, and it was he who then added the words 'fear of life' to his professional opinion of him.

This 'fear of life' prevented them from even consummating their marriage, and Billy, as the years progressed, became the baby that Bess never had. He spent his last years, after he retired from his job at the railway bogie works up at Heaton, wearing a nappy, and watching horse racing on his TV.

One of Bess's proudest claims was that because Billy worked on the railways, their free tickets entitled them to travel 'anywhere in England – free of charge!' Sadly, they did not take much advantage of this benefit, rarely going anywhere, although on their honeymoon, they went to Ireland and visited the Ring of Kerry.

That very same Dr Martin – how he seems to have had such a profound influence on everybody's life - also cautioned my grandma against having any more children after she had Agnes, my mam. One was enough for her, he said, and my grandma obeyed.

With their dyed-in-the-wool Victorian attitudes to everything firmly in place, I doubt that his advice would have allowed for much recreational sex either. I got the impression, in the one conversation I ever had with my grandma about their personal lives, that Dr Martin's advice had been taken very seriously.

My Uncle John never had a serious romantic relationship with anybody – or any kind of sexual encounter. True, there were the odd copies of 'Titbits' and 'Reveille' that he kept in his always locked bedroom, along with his very dangerous looking UV 'health' lamp, but that doesn't stack up to much of a sex life.

I suspect that the 'family chin' - or lack of chin - played some part in this. Thankfully, the chin has escaped my children thus far (who knows what surprises await the next generation?), but it defined John's face and all thoughts that he might wish to share - into one single expression – pure misery!

However, there was one brief romantic encounter that might or might not have happened. Whenever I find myself thinking about this one incident in John's life, I think about Samuel Beckett's play, 'Krapp's Last Tape', and of the parallels with this play that seem to both enhance and diminish the incident.

The play's only character, Krapp, remembers one incident, the most important incident in his life. He once watched a woman throw a ball for her dog. The ball came near to him and he almost – almost – talked to the woman – or the dog, but did neither. Instead, he makes tape recordings of his memories of that incident and plays them to himself incessantly.

It starts with the fifteen-year-old John becoming apprenticed as a fitter, walking to work with his dad in the same shipyard. He had signed up for five years of slave labour and monstrously low rates of pay, but there was the promise of a well-paid job as a 'time served' fitter at the end of it.

At this time, the fourth year of an apprenticeship offered the chance of excitement for most young men. That was the year when all the apprentices went to sea for a full year, and John's voyage was to be on a ship called 'Truro City'. I have a painting of that ship in my office now. It was one of the many ships commandeered by the UK government from Germany as reparations after the first world war. The Truro City was to take John to Australia, and to his one-time only chance to break away. John's 'Krapp moment' took place in Australia: he jumped ship.

He seems to have spent almost a year in and around Melbourne. He worked on a farm for much of that time, and it was on that farm that apparently, he met a girl. That was his one moment – his 'Krapp moment', and things might have been so very different had he made a different choice. But that very same 'moment' was completely banjaxed when he wrote home to his mother and asked her to pay his fare back to England.

He left Australia, and the girl, and returned to North Shields. From that moment on, he lived with his mother – and apart from a two day visit to Belfast on his one and only trip in an aircraft, proudly returning with a plastic BEA flight bag around his neck, that was it. He had done his living, and was doomed to rerun the tape of that one 'moment', of what might have been, for the rest of his life.

John eventually became a time-served fitter (his dad must have done some string pulling and got him to finish his apprenticeship). He became a very skilled man, and he worked in various shipyards up and down the Tyne until his sixty-fifth birthday. He was the only person left working in his workshop – everyone else having been paid off as the work in the yards ground to a halt.

All those girls who had married during and after the first war eventually became widows. Those without children to tend to them in their final years had some difficulty. Belle was cared for by Margaret, her daughter, but my mam had died, so Jane had nobody. Charlotte, and Bess had no children and John was just there.

This is what happened. When Charlotte's husband, Tommy, died, she sold her house in Dale Road, West Monkseaton, and bought a flat in Cleveland Terrace, North Shields.

Tommy had been a ship's First Engineer for all his working life. He was away from home for ten months of the year. After he retired, he realised that his was not a very happy marriage, and their last few years together were ones of open warfare.

After my grandad died, Jane and John lived together for some years in Lansdowne Terrace. When Jane died, John moved with his sister Bess into sheltered accommodation which they shared for some happy years.

It eventually fell to me to be the one to move Charlotte into a care home – very much against her will - when she became unable to look after herself. I had to do the same with Jane and John, as well as with my Aunt Bess who proved to be particularly difficult, as two care homes threw her out because she was so disruptive.

I tried to visit these oldies as often as I could, but it was never enough. And when John, the last one, died, that was the end of our relationship with North Shields.

My wife Wendy and I have lived in the Lake District for most of our adult lives, and all our children have been brought up in the magnificent Lakeland landscapes. We did live briefly in Switzerland and in Singapore, and my work continues to take me to many countries, but when I get back to my home, any journey that I have made, no matter how fraught with difficulty, is always worthwhile.

The title of these stories, 'Geordie Boy' could be seen to be a bit of a con because I don't live there now, and you may think that I may not qualify. Not true. Rather in the same way that 'Scottishness' seems to be best celebrated in Canada or Australia, being Geordie has been a badge that I have carried proudly all my life.

Now our visits to Tynemouth and North Shields are for pleasure, and I feel I could live there again. These are attractive places to live – now, and if the council manages to restore the open-air swimming pool at the southern end of the Longsands beach, a trip to the new Lido, followed by a leisurely meal at the Seafood Cabin, or in one of the many excellent restaurants on the Fish Quay, would be an attractive proposition to me – and to anyone else.

That feeling of wanting to return is a very recent phenomenon. I had to endure a long catharsis before it became possible. I have eventually been purged of the bile and resentment that built up in me during, what was a very difficult childhood and adolescence.

At that time, the whole of the shipbuilding world in the UK was coming to an end, and my great uncle John's retirement seems to have coincided with the end of the great yards: Smith's Dock, where he was working when he retired, Parson's, Reyrolle's, Walker's, North Eastern Marine – all great names, but from a long dead past.

At one point, the idea was for me also to follow on the tradition, and to take an apprenticeship in the yards myself (their idea, not mine), but as the shipbuilding industry was dying on its feet, and I was resolutely set on escaping North Shields, any arguments that might have been advanced to persuade me lacked credibility.

I do look back on my Geordie upbringing with mixed feelings – I still have the twang, which I modify into a kind of standard English for my videos and my seminars. For many years, my memories of Tyneside were so uniformly negative that 'anywhere but Tynemouth' was my mantra.

Now it is not the case – I could live there again – perhaps even on the Fish Quay, in the apartments of the old Tyne Brand building – or in the new development at what was Smith's Dock.

It's never going to happen – it's just a dream, but it is a dream that I am now able to consider – theoretically, at least, although both

Wendy, and now my grandkids, would certainly have something to say about that.

Before we settled our family in the Lakes, I had worked briefly as an actor and as a Drama Adviser. I then taught in two international schools, in Geneva and in Singapore, and in two universities, in Lancaster and Leeds.

We always wanted to run our own business, and not work for an employer. The Lakes was the place where both of us wanted to live. We tried, unsuccessfully it turns out, to develop a hotel company. It had two largish properties before it crashed and burned in a recession where bank base rates reached fifteen percent (yes, fifteen percent – and those days could return!). We had to liquidate our assets and start again.

But we did, and we did not give up. I am particularly thankful that our family was strong enough to stick together during what was a very difficult time. Wendy restarted her teaching career, and she worked in schools that catered for secondary age children with special needs – and perversely – she loved it.

Our children all were able to enjoy a great education at an excellent comprehensive school, and as I have said, all went to university. They all have made many friends who are still important to them and, the best thing of all – my kids are great friends with each other! This means that our regular family gatherings – where up to twenty of us can be present – are truly happy occasions.

I developed and now run a small management consultancy. I write and deliver my own business seminars in many soft-skill topic areas. I also write and present seminars for a company based in Dubai, which has sent me to many Middle Eastern countries as well as to cities all over India.

For many years, I have also worked with American seminar companies which employ me to present their material to their clients. In a period of about twenty-five years, I have presented business seminars to hundreds of companies and organisations in over twenty countries including Japan, Ukraine and Croatia.

Six of my business seminars can now be accessed via the internet, and the German company which invited me to record them reports steady progress in their various markets.

We also have a niche in professional sports Outplacement, and for over twenty years, we have had a strong relationship with the Professional Footballers' Association. We assist PFA members in making the transition from professional sport and into alternative careers – and very successfully too.

It has been a privilege for us being able to live in the centre of the Lake District for most of our adult lives. I must travel – sometimes thousands of miles – to deliver my seminars (I think of Preston, Manchester, Edinburgh and Leeds as 'local' when I obtain engagements in these cities), but that late night ride home in the car from Manchester airport - or especially from Newcastle airport, when I deliberately choose to drive back home along the Military Road, tells me exactly why I do what I do.

I arrive home, and I listen to the absolute silence of our valley, and our lifestyle choice is absolutely justified – we have made the right decision!

Printed in Poland
by Amazon Fulfillment
Poland Sp. z o.o., Wrocław